The Two-Edged Sword

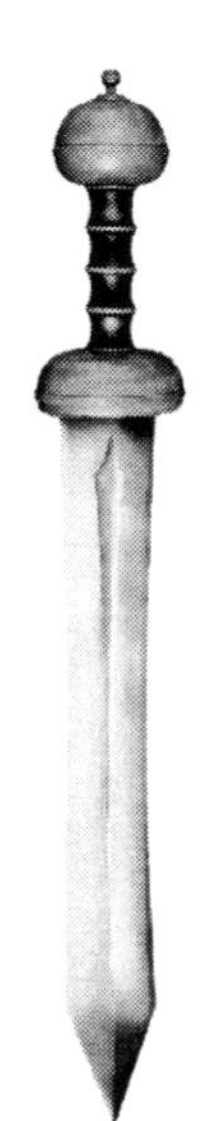

The Two-Edged Sword

Take the Journey with Benjamin
and let the Lord lead the way.
Blessings,
Caye Patterson Bartell
2014

By Caye Patterson Bartell

www.lifesentencepublishing.com
The Two-Edged Sword - Caye Patterson Bartell

Copyright © 2014

All rights reserved. No part of this book may be reproduced, stored in a retrieval system, or transmitted in any form or by any means - electronic, mechanical, photocopying, recording, or otherwise - without written permission from the publisher.

Some scripture quotations taken from the St Joseph Edition of The New American Bible. Copyright © 1970 by The Confraternity of Christian Doctrine, Washington, D.C., including the Revised New Testament, © 1986, is reproduced herein by license of said Confraternity of Christian doctrine. All rights reserved.

All other materials, including maps and illustrations, Copyright © 1987, 1980, 1970 by Catholic Book Publishing Co., New York, N.Y. Printed in the United States of America

Some scripture quotations taken from the New American Standard Bible®, Copyright © 1960, 1962, 1963, 1968, 1971, 1972, 1973, 1975, 1977, 1995 by The Lockman Foundation Used by permission. (www.Lockman.org)

Printed in the United States of America

First edition published 2014

LIFE SENTENCE Publishing books are available at discounted prices for ministries and other outreach.
Find out more by contacting us at info@lifesentencepublishing.com

LIFE SENTENCE Publishing and its logo are trademarks of

LIFE SENTENCE Publishing, LLC
P.O. Box 652
Abbotsford, WI 54405

Paperback ISBN: 978-1-62245-172-2

Ebook ISBN: 978-1-62245-173-9

10 9 8 7 6 5 4 3 2 1

This book is available from www.amazon.com, Barnes & Noble, and your local Christian bookstore.

Cover Design: Amber Burger

Editor: Katherine Keefer

Share this book on Facebook

Contents

The Word of the Lord is living and active
and sharper than a two-edged sword.
(Hebrews 4:12)

In Gratitude

From the first time I sat down at my computer to write *The Two-Edged Sword* until the last draft was completed, the Holy Spirit guided me and directed the book. If it were not for Him, then this young adult novel would not have been written. At the beginning of each chapter, when I prayed where to go next, the ideas came, as if out of nowhere, from this mighty source.

The Legend of the Dogwood Tree

Over 2000 years ago, the dogwood tree grew tall, strong, and sturdy like the oak tree. Then one was cut down, and the wooden beams were used for Jesus' cross.

Since that time, the tree no longer grows stately, but is slender, bent, and twisted. Its white flowers are shaped like crosses, and have small brown marks on each petal that look like bloodstains. The cluster of berries in the center of the flower resembles Christ's crown of thorns.

Acknowledgements

Each time I prayed for someone to critique, edit, or read my manuscript, God would send a friend willing to help.

One of the friends to put fingerprints on the early pages was Barb Smith, who not only read it once, but three times from start to finish. Her editing skills challenged me to see the sights and listen for the sounds that were going on around the characters, which helped the scenes come alive. My friend, Kim Parsons, edited the complete story twice. With her exceptional talent, she left her fingerprints throughout the chapters. Her recommendations to enhance or delete certain passages improved the story tremendously.

In addition to Barb and Kim, other friends have left fingerprints as well: Sue Swieciak, who offered suggestions along the way that added flavor; Deb DiSandro's read-through and input enriched many pages. Nancy Christman spent days with me reading the manuscript out-loud, looking for errors. My daughter Mary Ellen's keen insight allowed me to recognize some details in the journey with the Holy Spirit that might lead readers to misunderstand my intentions. Her help encouraged me to rewrite those sections.

Special thanks to those friends who read and made suggestions to both improve the story and correct my grammar: This includes all the above people, as well as: Judy Bartell, Helen Steil, and Gail Toerpe. In addition, thanks to my niece, Laura, who listened while I read the whole story as she drove me back from Superior.

Thanks goes to those at Red Bird Studio and Writer's Ink who critiqued some of the early chapters; the instructors and students at the Green Lake Christian Writers Conference; and the Road Scholar's "Exploring the Writer in You" leadership that helped shape me as a writer.

Of course, a big thanks (hugs and kisses) to my husband Jim, for his love and support in all my endeavors. To him and our children: Jimmy, Mary, Tony, and Nicole; their spouses: Judy, Mike, Sara, and Tim; and our grandchildren: Liza, Sarah, Ryan, Lexie, Lauren, and Emma. I love you all a lot. You are the blessings in my life.

Also in memory of my first teachers: my parents, Catherine and George; my brothers, Jerry, George, and Earl; my sister Joan, and especially my sister Maryann, who knew I could do it – thanks sis!

For all those who sent prayers for the completion of this book, I give thanks. If I've missed thanking anyone, forgive me, the Lord knows your name.

The final fingerprints are Jeremiah's and those at Life Sentence Publishing whose exceptional editing, design and layout made the book a reality.

This novel is a work of fiction created around events in the life of Jesus Christ.

ONE

THE UPRISING

Roman soldiers strutted along the upper walkway of the limestone wall that towered over Jerusalem. In their rugged hands, they carried sharp long-handled spears. Red tunics and leather breastplates decorated their muscular bodies. Atop their heads, brass helmets glinted in the sun.

At the North Gate, people flocked into the city.

In the middle of the crowd, Benjamin walked beside his mother and gave a quick nod toward the soldiers. “Look at the troops walking the wall, they circle above us like vultures waiting to pick our bones clean.”

“Hush, Son. The governor, Pilate, has spies everywhere. We must be careful.”

Benjamin inhaled deeply and puffed out his chest. “I’m not afraid.”

“I know you’re brave. That’s what worries me. But you’re just a young boy.” She reached up and tousled his dark curly hair.

He pulled away. "Mother, please. I know you mean well, but I'm thirteen. I'm a man."

She smiled and nodded. "Yes, you're taller than me now, that's true. But it's hard for me to believe you've grown so quickly."

Soldiers stationed at the gate's entrance used their long-handled spears to control the crowd. They jabbed and prodded, yelling, "Move along! Move along!"

Benjamin grasped his mother's arm. "Don't worry, Mother. Stay close. I'll keep you safe."

She patted his hand. "I know you're strong enough to protect me, but we better move quickly – those soldiers will show us no mercy."

Ignoring her warning, he paused and glanced around. "Soldiers are everywhere. They're at the gate, along the wall, and in the crowd. Something's wrong. I wonder what's going on?"

"It's not for us to question what they do." She tugged the sleeve of his tunic. "Let's keep moving or we'll draw their attention."

An uneasy feeling gripped Benjamin. "Mother, are you sure you want to shop this morning?"

"I came to buy cloth for your father's new cloak. I'll not leave without it. I'd like it finished before the baby's born."

With a heavy sigh, he continued to hold her arm as they made their way down the cobblestone street to the marketplace. Her stride had become cumbersome. Benjamin, smiling to himself, prayed that once the baby came, maybe she'd quit thinking of him as a child.

At the market, shoppers crowded both sides of the street. They swarmed to wooden booths stacked high with fruits and vegetables, clay pots, straw baskets and fine textiles. Customers haggled with merchants who argued back.

When Benjamin and his mother passed a booth lined with fragrant oils, a woman standing there called out, "Good morning, Hannah. It's a fine day for shopping."

Mother nodded. "Yes, it is, Martha."

The sweet smell of honey and pungent spices hung in the air. One merchant, selling large purple grapes shouted, "Fresh from a neighboring vineyard. Juicy enough to clear the dust from your throat!"

Mother shoved a coin into Benjamin's hand. "Go buy some for us. I'll check the fabric booth across the way. I'm sure they'll have what I want."

"Father told me not to let you wander off by yourself."

"You and your father fret needlessly."

"But I'm not to leave you alone."

"Don't worry. I'll be all right." She tucked a loose strand of her dark hair under her white headscarf, turned, and walked away.

A shiver surged through Benjamin. Why doesn't she ever listen?

On the other side of the street, a beggar with an outstretched hand approached his mother. Benjamin knew she couldn't afford to give anything. Nevertheless, she dropped something into the man's hand. Benjamin couldn't help grinning at her generosity as he went off to buy the fruit.

He bought a large bunch of grapes and popped some into his mouth. As he chomped, he pictured how his life would change once the baby was born. Then without warning, a thunderous stomping shocked him back from his daydreaming.

Soldiers were marching into the marketplace, their metal-tipped spears positioned for battle. The soldier in the lead wielded a two-edged sword.

Shouts rang out from the far end of the street. A band of renegades rushed into the square. Benjamin had heard about these rebels - militant Jews determined to overthrow the Roman government that ruled in Jerusalem. Armed with crude wooden clubs, they raced toward the soldiers. The sudden clash of weapons sent shoppers screaming and running in all directions.

Benjamin threw down his grapes. A fight broke out near him, and he frantically scanned the area looking for his mother. He saw her crouched next to a booth piled high with fabrics.

"Mother!" he shouted.

She stood up and started toward him, paying no attention to the fight going on around her.

"Stay where you are! Stay where you are!" he called. He tried to cross over to her, but a hefty man fell against him, knocking him into a booth heaped with persimmons. The red fruit spilled to the ground and rolled across the cobblestones. Benjamin leapt over them, landing among a few renegades who were fighting fiercely with soldiers.

As he tried to find a way out, the wooden handle of a spear grazed his forehead and knocked him backward. He collided with a broad-shouldered rebel.

A crude grunt spilled from the rebel's mouth. His wild eyes glared. He raised a hand that was the size of a bear's paw and cuffed Benjamin alongside the head. "You're a feeble excuse for a Jew. Be a man, get into the fight!"

The rebel seized the front of Benjamin's tunic and threw him into the thick of the battle. The air reeked of sweat and blood. The bruise on Benjamin's forehead throbbed. He didn't want to fight, he just wanted to find his mother and get her out of there.

He searched the crowd again, and saw her staggering in a daze amid the upheaval. Some fighters blocked his way. Shoving through them, he found himself right behind the soldier who had led the troops. He was swinging his two-edged sword wildly.

"Be prepared to die, Barabbas," the soldier shouted, and lunged forward, his sword aimed at the rebel who had cuffed Benjamin.

The rebel, Barabbas, leapt aside. Benjamin gasped as his mother stepped into the path of the menacing blade. The metal tip plunged into her side. She slumped to the ground.

"No!" He heard himself scream.

Determined to get to her, he pushed aside everyone in his path. Benjamin wanted a glimpse of the soldier's face so he could identify him later, but he had already disappeared into a group of fighters.

When Benjamin reached his mother, he dropped to his knees. She was clutching the wound with her right hand. Blood seeped through her fingers. All around them, rebels and soldiers were still engaged in the battle.

"Son, you've been hurt."

He had forgotten about his bruised forehead.

"I'm all right. It's you who needs help."

He placed an arm firmly around her waist and lifted her to her feet. She leaned against him as he led her behind a nearby booth, and there he sat her down. Her headscarf was missing. Her black hair hung loose. How could he have let this happen? He should have stayed with her. What if she died?

His heart thumped as if it were coming through the front of his tunic. "Mother, I have to get you to the physician's house."

"No, Son, I want to go home."

"But if the bleeding doesn't stop..."

"Hush, do as I ask."

"But I must get help."

Her dark eyes were wet with tears as she pleaded, "Take me to your father."

"All right, if that's what you want, but first let me tie my sash where you've been stabbed. The pressure will stop the bleeding." He took off his cloth belt and wrapped it around her midsection.

Their house was only a short distance down the hill from the city, but he worried that once they were home there wouldn't be anyone who could care for his mother's wound.

He peered over the edge of the booth. The battle that raged moments ago ended as suddenly as it had begun. Soldiers were carrying their fallen comrades down the side street toward the barracks at Antonia Fortress. Rebels who had survived the skirmish were fleeing the scene.

The dead and injured lay scattered on the cobblestone streets between overturned booths and debris. Groans from the wounded created an eerie sound.

Mother's eyes, once sparkling with laughter, were dulled by pain.

Benjamin prayed silently, "God, if you let her and the baby live, I'll continue to study the Torah and become a devoted rabbi like my father. I'll serve you faithfully all the days of my life."

He helped his mother to stand. "Are you sure you can make it?" he asked tenderly.

She nodded, leaning against him. They moved cautiously around women who had earlier run from the marketplace, but who now returned to care for their fallen loved ones.

The city streets were empty. Benjamin noticed people peering at them from doorways. Struck with fear by the uprising, they offered no help, and were quick to dart back inside their work places.

At the North Gate, the few soldiers still on guard turned away, paying them no attention.

Outside the city wall, the dirt road seemed to stretch endlessly before them. The rutted roadway was littered with loose stones. Benjamin's steps were unsteady as he held up his mother. In the distance, he could see the outer edge of his grandfather's olive grove.

A herd of sheep, guided by a lone shepherd and his barking dog, passed in front of them, stirring up dust. Mother began to cough and choke on the fine powder. "I can't make it," she whispered.

Then the thatched roof of their stone house came into view.

"Don't worry, Mother," Benjamin said, holding her closer. "We're almost home."

TWO

THE AFTERMATH

Benjamin hurried to the house with his mother leaning heavy against his side. The muscles in his arms and legs ached and burned like hot cinders. "Father, help! Help me!"

The front door flew open. Father rushed outside, his long black robe flapping in the wind. His dark eyes were wide with fear. "What happened to your mother?"

"She's hurt. A battle broke out in the city between soldiers and renegades. She was stabbed and wouldn't let me take her to the physician's house."

Father, slipping her from Benjamin's grasp, lifted her into his arms. "Hannah, everything is going to be all right."

She smiled up at him.

"Son, go quickly into the city and fetch the physician. He will know what to do." Deep lines of concern were etched in Father's face.

As Benjamin ran, his sandaled feet slapped against

the deserted road. His sweat-soaked tunic stuck to his back, and his breath came in quick gulps. Before he entered the North Gate, he slowed down. The few soldiers still on duty paid him no attention.

When he reached the physician's house, he pounded his fist on the large wooden door. The minute it opened, he grabbed the man's hand. "Come quickly, my mother was stabbed during an uprising in the marketplace, and the bleeding won't stop."

"I just found out about the battle," the physician said. "My sons went on ahead of me to help. I was to follow. But considering your mother's condition, I'll go with you instead. Give me a minute to finish gathering my things. Then you can tell me everything."

They were soon out the door, and as they hurried down the road, Benjamin explained the uprising and all that had taken place. At the house, they went inside into his parent's bedroom. Father was kneeling next to the bed where Mother lay.

Grandfather was already in the room, standing behind Father. His tattered brown robe hung loose on his body. In his thick weathered hand, he gripped a lit oil lamp and moved next to Benjamin while the physician began examining Mother's wound.

"I heard your shouts for help while I was working in the olive grove," Grandfather said. "I came to the house right away, but you had already left."

"Grandfather, do you think she'll be all right?"

"We can only pray. Let's step into the outer room.

They'll come for us as soon as the physician finishes his examination." He placed the oil lamp on a stand near the bed.

In the center of the main room, Benjamin slumped down on a floor cushion at their long wooden table. He told Grandfather everything that had happened in the city. After he finished, he buried his head in his hands. It seemed like forever before the physician came out of the bedroom with Father. "I'm afraid there is nothing I can do," he said quietly.

Benjamin ran to his father and grabbed his sleeve. "Do something, Father. You're a rabbi. Pray that she lives."

"I have prayed. Now your mother and the baby are in God's hands."

Benjamin's jaw tightened. Hadn't God heard his earlier prayer? What good were prayers if they were not answered?

"I'd better leave and go to the marketplace," the physician said as he headed for the door. "They still may need my help."

Father showed him out. No one spoke as they all went back into the bedroom. Father again knelt by Mother's bed. Grandfather, his back rigid, stood behind him. Benjamin sat close to the bed, watching his mother's every breath.

"Mother, please don't die," he whispered.

She smiled at him, reached over, and touched his

hand. Hers was cold. She closed her eyes. Her breathing became more and more labored until it finally stopped.

"Mother? Mother?" Benjamin called out. It only took him a moment to realize she was dead. He knew what he must do. He gritted his teeth and tore at the top of his tunic until it ripped, exposing the area over his heart. He saw his father and grandfather doing the same with their garments. When his grandmother died last year, they had performed the same ritual out of love and respect for her. His love for his mother made his heart ache as if it had been torn along with his tunic.

Tears pooled in his eyes, but he squeezed them shut so he wouldn't cry. He was no longer a child. Then he heard his father and grandfather moaning and sobbing, and his eyes flew open. They were grown men, but that didn't stop them from expressing their grief.

Still, he bit down on his lower lip, refusing to let go of the anger he held toward God for not saving his mother.

Father wiped his eyes on his sleeve, and leaned down to kiss Mother's forehead. "My dearest Hannah. My beloved wife," he said. He slowly stood, bowed his head, and began to pray, "Lord our God, King of the Universe. I know there is a time for everything under the sun. A time to live and a time to..." He stopped speaking and placed his hands over his face.

Grandfather, choking out the words, continued the prayer where Father left off. "A time to die. A time to sow and a time to reap. A time..."

Benjamin blocked out the rest of what Grandfather was saying. He set his jaw firmly. God hadn't listened to his prayer. Why should he listen to the words spoken from the Torah? He wanted to run from the room, but his legs were as heavy as boulders. In silence, he sat with his head bowed.

Grandfather finished the prayer and touched Father's shoulder. "Samuel, we have to lay Hannah and the baby to rest before sunset. Benjamin will come with me to get spices to anoint the body."

Not looking up, Father nodded.

Even though his legs were heavy, Benjamin rose and followed his grandfather. The old man went to a large wooden cupboard near a clay oven at the far end of the other room. He took out a jar of myrrh and one of aloe and gave them to his grandson. "Hold these while I get some linen cloth to wrap the body."

The sweet-spicy smells made Benjamin's stomach queasy. "I feel sick, Grandfather. Is it alright if I wait outside until you're done?"

"We need you to hold the lamp for us."

With his shoulders slouched, Benjamin walked back into the bedroom. He handed his father the spices while Grandfather laid the white linens next to the body.

"Benjamin, pick up the oil lamp," Grandfather said as he began to assist Father with the anointing.

Gripping the lamp in his hands, Benjamin stared into the orange glow. An image of the soldier plunging the sword into his mother's side danced in the inner flame. Benjamin felt as if the sword was piercing his own body, and he grabbed his side.

"We need more light." Grandfather's voice shook Benjamin out of his trance. The sword hadn't stabbed him. It was only his imagination, but his mother's death was real.

"Son, bring the lamp closer," Father said softly.

Benjamin inched toward the bed. Light spread across the partially wrapped body. His hands started to shake. Why couldn't he control them? He was brave – his mother had told him so.

"Hold the lamp still." Father reached over to steady Benjamin's hands.

"It's my fault she's dead." Benjamin's lower lip quivered. "I shouldn't have left her to buy grapes. If I had stayed with her, she and the baby would be alive."

Deep lines furrowed Father's forehead. "That is not true!"

"But you told me to stay with her!"

"No, I should have gone with her into the city. If anyone is responsible—"

"Enough!" Grandfather shook his head. "My daughter loved you both. She would not want you to blame yourselves."

Benjamin clenched his hands tighter around the lamp. Grandfather's right, it was the soldier's fault, he and his two-edged sword. And God – God did nothing to stop it. Still, he couldn't shake the shame of his own actions.

Grandfather walked to the door. "Benjamin, set the lamp on the stand and go with me to get the cart."

He did as Grandfather asked. They went to a stone hut behind the house and dragged out a hand-drawn cart. After they pushed it around to the front door, Father came out carrying the shrouded body. He laid it carefully on the wooden boards.

Benjamin and his father each took hold of a long side handle and pulling together, they moved down the deserted road toward the burial grounds. Grandfather walked next to them with his head down.

The wheels creaked and groaned as they hit deep ruts. Benjamin felt like he was walking in a bad dream.

Before dusk, they approached the ground level burial sites outside Jerusalem. This was where the poor buried their dead. Families were weeping and wailing over the bodies of their loved ones. Benjamin wondered if they were killed in the uprising too.

The family tomb was built into a terraced hillside. Usually, only the rich could afford such a grand burial site, but last year when Grandmother died, Grandfather, deep in mourning, insisted on buying the finest tomb he could afford.

They made their way up the hill. Outside the tomb, various sized rocks were wedged around a large wheel-like boulder that blocked the entrance. Grandfather and Benjamin removed them, and with the help of Father, they shoved against the boulder, rolling it away.

Without delay, Father lifted the shrouded body and carried it into the tomb. It was dark and damp. The air was stale and musty. Father placed Mother's body on a gray slab next to Grandmother's. Once Benjamin's eyes adjusted to the darkness, he saw Grandfather's shaky hand resting on Grandmother's shrouded remains. "It'll be all right, Grandfather," he whispered, wanting to comfort him, but knowing his words sounded hollow.

"With the loss of your grandmother last year, and now my daughter's death, it's too much to bear." Tears wet the old man's weathered face and slid into his beard. Still too angry to cry, Benjamin clenched his teeth and swallowed his grief.

Although his father's lips were moving in prayer, Benjamin didn't hear the words. His thoughts went to the soldier and the two-edged sword. Even though he hadn't seen the soldier's face, maybe he could recognize the sword if he saw it again. But did all the swords look the same?

Father nudged him. "Son, it is time to leave."

Benjamin looked at the remains of his mother one last time. A stabbing pain burned in his chest. He turned away and left the tomb.

Outside, a deep breath of fresh air cleared his lungs. He helped his father and grandfather replace the boulder at the opening.

Grandfather picked up a rock. "Let's make sure the tomb's secure. Jackals are known to squeeze through the smallest holes."

The thought of wild animals attacking his mother's body made Benjamin shudder. He quickly packed rocks into any opening. Father lifted one of the cart's handle, and Benjamin grabbed the other one. They walked side by side, pulling the empty cart toward home. Grandfather, his shoulders hunched, followed behind.

They stopped at the cistern on their return where they filled a clay waterpot and prepared to wash. It was a way to purify themselves after handling Mother's lifeless body.

When they finished, the cart was put away. Once inside the house, a cold chill shot through Benjamin. Usually when he came home, Mother was at the oven, the smell of her freshly baked bread filling the room. She'd smile and give him a warm hug. Now, feeling cold and empty, he dropped down onto a floor cushion at the table.

"We are all tired," Father said, rubbing his temple. "But before we turn in we should eat. After the meal is over, we will recite evening prayers like always."

Benjamin got up slowly. "I'm not hungry."

"Would you check to see if I left any of my tools in the olive grove?" Grandfather asked as he winked affectionately at Benjamin.

Why was Grandfather sending him out to the olive grove so late?

"I wouldn't want them left out overnight," Grandfather said as he winked again.

Then Benjamin remembered – after Grandmother's death, Grandfather would go alone to the edge of the olive grove in the evening and sit under his beloved dogwood tree. He said it gave him time to think and clear his mind.

"All right, Grandfather, I'll go and check."

Father sighed and shook his head. "Do not be gone long. We need our sleep. By tomorrow, the neighbors will have heard the news. They will come early in the morning to express their condolences and pray with us."

Benjamin had forgotten that there would be a seven-day period of mourning. When his grandmother died, the neighbors came to pray with the family. They brought food and sat quietly without speaking unless they were spoken to first. Some women, unable to keep in their grief, wept softly. Father and Grandfather only spoke when reciting ritual prayers of mourning, and the silence became unbearable for Benjamin. He didn't look forward to the days ahead and would be glad when they were over.

He left the house and walked down the path. If people came in the morning, he could pretend to pray with them, and no one would know how he really felt.

The moon lit the way to the olive grove. At the dogwood tree, he dropped down and leaned against the rough bark. Voices of past conversations with Father and Mother echoed in his ears. The three of them spent many hours under the tree together, talking, laughing, and planning his future as a rabbi. Now, he didn't even want to think about that. Those days ended the second his mother died.

A chilly wind blew through the olive grove. Black clouds drifted in front of the moon. Benjamin, choking out the words, shouted into the darkness, "God, the Torah says you care about your people, but it lies! You don't care! If you did, Mother and the baby would have lived. I'll never become a rabbi and serve you. And I'll never ask anything from you again!"

THREE

BENJAMIN AND THE ROMAN SOLDIER

As the heat of the sun beat down on Benjamin's back, he yawned and rubbed his eyes. He headed for the shed behind the house, exhausted from another restless night.

The mourning period for his mother had ended weeks ago, but nightmares of her stabbing and death had crept into his sleep. He would wake in the middle of the night, trembling. He couldn't shake the feeling of shame that haunted him day and night. If only he hadn't let her go off alone.

Inside the shed, he fumbled through the tools on the shelf until he found a pruning knife. The wooden handle felt heavy in his hands. He carefully slid his fingertips along the blade. It was dull and needed sharpening. At the grinding wheel, he dropped down onto the seat.

With the blade's edge placed against the stone, he pumped the pedal until sparks flew. Once it was sharpened, he stuck the knife into the cloth sash wrapped around his waist and headed for the olive grove.

Rows and rows of trees needed trimming. Not knowing where to begin, Benjamin zigzagged through them, checking each one. He found a tree with only a few dead branches. It seemed like a good place to start.

He removed the knife from the sash and slipped the blunt side of the blade between his teeth. His hand grabbed the lowest branch on the tree. Then he swung his long legs over it, pulled up, and scrambled to the top.

After he removed the pruning knife from his mouth, he placed the sharp edge against a dead branch and sawed. The blade cut through, and the branch spiraled downward. It hit the ground and splintered.

He leaned back against the trunk. If only the soldier who had killed his mother could be destroyed as easily, maybe his nightmares would end.

A burst of light flashed through the leaves. The brightness was blinding. Benjamin blinked a few times, rubbed his eyes, and searched for the source.

Next to the road, a tall Roman soldier stood beneath one of the olive trees. He was staring into the grove, the sunlight bouncing off his brass helmet. A long red cape draped over his body. The large black pack slung over his left shoulder looked heavy. Benjamin knew if this man discovered him, he would be forced to carry his gear – Roman soldiers were known to treat Jews like their personal slaves.

Where was Grandfather? He was supposed to work

in the grove today. Was he at the cistern getting water? If so, Benjamin had to warn him about the intruder.

Without stirring, Benjamin waited. Sweat beaded on his forehead. The soldier didn't budge; he remained standing under the shade tree.

Then, with a swift movement, the intruder swung his pack to his right shoulder and turned around to look up the road toward Jerusalem. With the man's back to him, Benjamin knew if he were to escape, now was the time.

He dropped the knife to the ground, slid to a lower branch and leaped down. Landing with a thud, he was quick to dart behind a tree. A few moments passed before he peered out to see if he had been heard.

The intruder was shifting his pack again. His arms bulged, and his thick leg muscles rippled.

Benjamin glanced over at the long stone wall that separated the grove from the house. The cistern was situated on the far side of the dwelling. If he could reach the wall without being seen, he could leap over it and run to warn his grandfather.

He crawled forward on his belly. The ground was hard and dry beneath his hands. Stones dug into his knees. A black scorpion scurried out from under a nearby rock, its poisonous tail pointed at him. Picking up a slender stick, he poked the vermin and forced it to scurry away.

Would the soldier ever leave? Benjamin was afraid to look, but he had to risk it. He lifted his head slowly. The intruder wasn't by the tree, but instead, he was walking straight at him.

Had he been seen? The rapid beat of Benjamin's heart thumped in his ears. He raised his head again. The soldier was getting closer, but for some reason, he stopped abruptly and flipped back his cape. Beneath it, a black sheath hung from a wide brass belt at his waist. The polished handle of a two-edged sword stuck out of the top of the sheath, and his rugged hand rested on it. Could that be the sword that stabbed Mother? He couldn't tell for sure. Maybe it was, but a number of soldiers carried swords.

Although he despised the dreadful weapon, Benjamin longed to get a better look. Of course, that would be foolish. The dogwood tree nearby was the perfect place to hide. He darted behind its thick trunk and listened for footsteps, but none came. The waiting became intolerable, and he peeked out.

There, just inches from his face, the sharp tip of the sword flashed in the sunlight. His eyes trailed the thick blade up to the handle where the soldier glared down at him. A slender purple scar ran from the edge of the man's right eye to the corner of his upper lip.

Benjamin trembled, but he couldn't stop staring. Was he looking at the man who killed his mother? With their helmets on, all soldiers looked alike. And the scar – it hadn't been visible from a distance, but now with the man so close, it was hard to miss.

"So, you thought you could hide from me? You're not quick enough." The soldier tossed his large pack at Benjamin's feet. "Here, boy, carry this."

Benjamin drew in a deep breath and stood up. "I'm not a boy. I'm a man."

"You're too scrawny to be a man."

"I'm thirteen."

"Well, if you're a man, you'll have no problem carrying my gear. Pick it up!"

"I can't. I'm working, pruning trees."

The soldier quickly slipped his sword back into its casing. "Did you hear me? I said carry my pack." He grabbed Benjamin's shoulders and shook him wildly, finally releasing him with a shove. Benjamin flew backwards, hitting his head on the trunk of the dogwood tree. The earth spun as he slid to the ground.

The soldier hunched over him. "Get up! Or you'll feel the edge of my sword." His eyes narrowed and his scar appeared to etch deeper into his cheek.

Benjamin rubbed his head, and let out a groan.

"When I tell you to do something, you'd better follow orders."

He would do what he was told, but it didn't mean he would like it.

The soldier turned and strutted toward the road. Benjamin struggled to his feet. He lifted the pack by its wide leather strap, flung it onto his right shoulder, and ran to catch up. He had no choice.

On the road, a donkey, weighted down with large bundles of wheat, brayed while its master prodded it along with a stick. A shepherd drove his flock toward the city with the help of a barking dog.

Dust flew up into Benjamin's eyes; he blinked as he tried to keep up with the soldier's long strides. The leather strap cut into his shoulder. He kept swinging the load from shoulder to shoulder until it slipped, and dropped to the ground with a thump.

The soldier spun around. "You clumsy Jew. I'll teach you never to mishandle my gear." Without hesitation, he pulled his sword from its sheath and jabbed the tip of it into Benjamin's right ankle.

A stinging pain shot up his leg, and blood trickled across his sandal. He bent down and covered the cut with the sleeve of his tunic. "Why did you stab me? I've done nothing wrong." He tried not to sound fearful.

"Quit complaining or I'll do worse the next time." The soldier wiped the blood off the tip of the sword with the end of his cape and slid it back into its casing. "Now, move quickly. I'm already late."

Benjamin knew he was no match for the soldier's sword, so he picked up the pack and followed.

Before they reached the city, the terraced hillside that held his family's tomb came into sight. An image of his mother's body lying inside flooded into his mind. His throat tightened, but he was determined not to show any sign of emotion since it would be thought of as another sign of weakness.

"Stop lagging," the soldier demanded.

Benjamin glanced one more time at the tomb before he focused his attention on the Jerusalem wall ahead. Travelers were entering the city at the North Gate.

Each year, pilgrims journeyed to Jerusalem from distant places like Caesarea, Nazareth, and Cana to worship at the temple during Passover. Since the feast was only a few days away, there would be a steady stream of them filing into the city for the sacred celebration.

The soldier strutted through the North Gate as people scrambled out of his way.

"Are we going to Antonia Fortress?" Benjamin asked, without thinking.

There was no response.

An old blind man stumbled into the soldier's path. With the force of his forearm, the soldier knocked him to the ground. "Out of my way!"

Benjamin stretched out a hand to help the old man up. The soldier hit it away. "Leave him alone, you insolent pup. He knows better than to bother one of Rome's finest."

With that said, he swaggered down the street that led to the Antonia Fortress. Benjamin followed reluctantly.

Soldiers were patrolling the upper wall of the army garrison that commanded a view of the Jewish temple. They marched between the high stone towers situated on each of the four corners.

Benjamin had never set foot beyond the large wooden gate, but he had heard about the bathhouses and luxurious quarters that housed the Roman soldiers.

Before they reached the entrance, Benjamin dropped the pack and leaned against a pile of limestone rocks stacked by the wall. He spit into his hands and rubbed some of the crusty, dry blood off his ankle.

"What are you doing?" The soldier was standing near the closed gate that led into the fortress. "I'm not through with you yet, boy. Bring my gear here."

"Coming!" Benjamin said, through clenched teeth.

As he hefted the pack onto his sore shoulder, the fortress gate swung wide and a husky young soldier strolled out. His smile drew attention to his large, square jaw.

"Marcus," he said. "I've been waiting for you. Where have you been? And what have we here?"

"Thaddeus, my friend, I've found a pack mule to carry my gear. He's stubborn, that's for certain, but I've tamed him."

"That's the only way to handle these headstrong Jews."

Marcus snatched his pack from Benjamin. "I'll see you again, boy. You can count on that." Without another word, Marcus and Thaddeus disappeared through the open gate.

Benjamin rubbed his aching shoulders. Why couldn't they find a way to drive these bullies from their land? Did they have to keep waiting for the promised Messiah, he who never comes?

A troop of soldiers came marching down the street. Benjamin ducked behind the pile of limestone rocks. He held his breath as they entered the Roman garrison. As soon as they went inside, he dashed back to the marketplace and made his way to the North Gate. Once outside the city walls, even though his ankle throbbed, Benjamin ran as fast as he could back to the olive grove.

FOUR

GRANDFATHER

On Benjamin's return to the olive grove, his grandfather, dressed in his frayed brown robe, waited in the shade of the dogwood tree at the edge of the road. His dark eyes appeared troubled. "Benjamin, where have you been? I was worried. What's that? Blood on your ankle?"

"A Roman soldier forced me to carry his gear into the city. Because I didn't move fast enough, he jabbed me with his sword."

"Well, at least you're all right," Grandfather said, stroking his beard, but then he sighed. "Will the Romans never leave us in peace? My whole life I've put up with these barbarians treating us like slaves. Now you have to live with their brutality, too. Will it ever end? If the Messiah would come, we could—"

"Do you really believe that God will send the Messiah?"

"I trust what the Torah teaches. God will keep his promise."

Benjamin shook his head. "God doesn't always answer prayers, and he doesn't keep his promises either."

"Don't blaspheme. The Messiah will come. And when he does, he'll gather an army who will fight to put an end to the Roman persecution. I pray it'll be soon."

"I don't know, Grandfather. I just don't know."

"Your father is anxious to go to the temple. He expects us to go with him."

Benjamin scuffed his sandal in the dirt. "Must I?"

"What do you mean? Of course you have to go with us."

"I can't worship at the temple anymore. God let Mother die."

Grandfather put his hand to his forehead. "How can you say that? The Lord didn't cause her death."

Benjamin could see that he had upset his grandfather, yet still, he had to speak. "But God didn't save her either. I prayed that Mother and the baby would live, and God refused to hear me."

"The hatred between the Romans and the Jews caused the uprising. A soldier killed your mother with his sword. You mustn't blame the Lord. We must remain strong in our faith. Our traditions and our worship in the temple are the only real freedoms we have left."

"I want to honor our customs, but to honor God, no. God doesn't care what happens to us. If He did, He would have sent the Messiah long ago."

"We don't always understand the ways of the Lord. His ways are greater than ours. As you continue your study of the Torah, you'll appreciate our faith and our heritage. Don't you want to become a rabbi like your father?"

"Why should I serve God? He doesn't care about me."

Grandfather rested his hand on the rough bark of the dogwood tree. "You know, as a young boy, I came with my parents from Tiberias to Jerusalem. I brought this tree as a seedling with me from Galilee. I planted it here, and look how it's grown. It's tall and straight and is a magnificent sight to behold."

Benjamin frowned and shook his head. "Grandfather, I love your stories about the dogwood tree, but please, not now."

Grandfather overlooked this plea and continued, "In the beginning, the seedling needed a lot of tender care to survive. As the years passed, it grew and its shade protected me from the hot sun. It provided me with a place to sit, rest, and resolve my problems. That's how our faith in the Lord grows. It starts out like a fragile seedling. As it blossoms and flourishes, it becomes a safe haven from life's difficulties. Do you understand?"

Benjamin shrugged. "But it doesn't change the way I feel. Nothing can change that."

"I know it's difficult for you without your mother, but she would not want you to become bitter and turn away from the Lord. I miss her too." Grandfather's eyes welled with tears.

Benjamin felt his throat tighten. Biting down on his lower lip, he refused to let go of his anger toward God.

"I'd better change my clothes," Grandfather said, wiping his wet eyes with his sleeve. "I'll let your father know we'll attend the service with him."

"Grandfather, I can't—"

"Listen to me. Stop at the cistern and clean the blood from your cut. Don't be long or your father will come looking for you."

After Grandfather left, Benjamin kicked a clump of dirt, sending broken pieces flying everywhere. He knew he'd obey his grandfather. He always did.

At the cistern, a clay waterpot with a wide opening lay next to it on the ground. He picked it up, tied a rope to one of its handles, and lowered it into the well. He pulled it up full to the brim and placed the smooth edge to his lips, drinking thirstily. Water spilled from the sides of his mouth and soaked the front of his tunic. Once his thirst was quenched, he lowered the pot again.

This time when he pulled it up, he peered into the water. The dark brown eyes that stared back at him reminded him of his mother's. The black curly hair matched his father's. Dunking his hand into the pot, he swished the water around, disrupting the image.

He washed the blood off his ankle, and sloshed his

bloody sleeve in the water until it was clean. He wiped his face with the wet sleeve as he headed for the house.

Before he entered the front door, some sacred verses from the Torah flashed through his mind. "Hear O Israel, the Lord is our God, the Lord is one. You shall love the Lord your God with all your heart, with all your soul, and with all your might. These words which I am commanding you today, shall be on your heart."

A feeling of emptiness washed over him. His heart was heavy as he realized those verses he had memorized with his father and mother were now meaningless. Why should he continue praying them? He didn't believe them anymore. He vowed he would never say them again. Sucking in a deep breath, he pushed opened the door and went inside.

His father sat on a floor cushion at the long wooden table. His head rested in his hands as if in prayer. The black robe he wore was draped with a white mourning shawl. A lock of his dark, wavy hair poked out from under a head-cloth that was held in place with a black band. His beard, though long, was neatly trimmed.

"Father, I'm here," Benjamin said, trying to act as if nothing was wrong.

His father looked up. "Where have you been? You had me worried."

"I'm sorry I'm late." Benjamin avoided his father's eyes, hoping he wouldn't notice the cut on his ankle.

"I am to assist at the service today. You know I like

to be on time. Son, your tunic is disgraceful. You cannot be seen at the temple dressed like that."

Benjamin wanted to tell him that he no longer cared to attend the service, but his father would never have understood.

Grandfather came from the bedroom he shared with Benjamin. He was dressed in his white temple robe. "Is it time to go, Samuel?"

"We will leave as soon as Benjamin changes his tunic. We will wait for him, but not for long."

Benjamin darted into the bedroom, pulled off his soiled tunic and loincloth, and dropped them on his cot. After grabbing clean clothing from a wooden shelf, he dressed quickly. He ran his fingers through his curly hair and then returned to the outer room.

Father stood and gave a nod of approval. Without saying another word, they left the house and headed for the temple on Mount Moriah.

FIVE

MOUNT MORIAH

With Passover a few days away, the number of people in the city streets had doubled. Pilgrims, their voices high-pitched with excitement, flocked to attend the afternoon service.

Benjamin trailed behind his father and grandfather. The excitement he used to feel during Passover was gone. This year, it wouldn't be the same without his mother. Passover would never be the same again.

The smells of fish, spices, and goat cheese in the air reminded him that he hadn't eaten since early morning. Booths that were damaged during the riot were now mended and piled high with food. With the thought of the uprising, his appetite disappeared.

"Shalom, Rabbi Samuel," a barley merchant called. "God has blessed us with good weather. The crops will be plentiful."

Father nodded politely.

"Shalom to you, too, Jacob," the merchant said. "Your grandson has grown this past year."

Grandfather smiled. "Yes, he's as tall as a stalk of wheat ready for the harvest."

Feeling his face growing hot, Benjamin stared down at the cobblestones and stepped from stone to stone. Unexpectedly, he bumped into his father.

Father turned to face him. "Son, watch where you are going."

A slight grin crossed Grandfather's face.

"Sorry, Father, but there – there's a pebble in my sandal. It's hurting my toe." Benjamin swallowed hard, ashamed that he had lied.

"Remove it and be quick. It is late. We will go on ahead. Meet us by the Nicanor Gate."

Bending down, he pretended to dig out the fictitious pebble. People pressed in around him. Out of the corner of his eye, he watched his father and grandfather head toward the outer courtyard of the temple. What would happen if he didn't follow? He'd have to lie again, and he couldn't do that. Once was enough.

After he stood up, he pushed through the growing crowd to the Nicanor Gate. Men surrounded the booths of the moneychangers and were haggling with the merchants who sold sacrificial doves and pigeons.

A large group gathered before the gate to the inner courtyard. They were talking loudly. Benjamin's friend Daniel was standing next to his father, Rabbi Aaron, at the far side of the yard. As usual, Daniel tugged at the neck of the tunic, which fit snuggly over his short, stocky body. His chubby face was covered with sweat.

Father and Grandfather stood discussing something with a group of men. They were all nodding and gesturing. When Benjamin joined them, Grandfather leaned over and motioned to the place where the women gathered. "Isn't that Daniel's twin sister, Rachel, with her mother? She's grown quite lovely."

Trying not to seem too eager to see her, Benjamin acted as if he hadn't heard. But as soon as Grandfather started speaking to Father, he searched the area until he spotted Rachel whispering to another girl. He couldn't take his eyes off her. She looked up and her dark eyes met his. He glanced away – embarrassed that she caught him staring.

Temple guards weaved in and out of the crowds. One bumped into Grandfather. "Lookout, old man," the guard snarled. He gave Grandfather another shove, and swaggered away.

"They're Jews same as us, but they're arrogant," Grandfather said. "It amuses them to use their power to keep us in line."

"Be careful," Father whispered. "You know they will arrest anyone who speaks out against their authority."

The large gate swung wide. Everyone surged forward. Benjamin was swept along into the Court of Israel. Even though he hadn't wanted to come, the sight of the magnificent temple with the majestic columns and long marble stairway made him proud to be a Jew.

As a young child, when his father took him to the temple, he had been in awe of the rituals. His father would hold onto his hand and say reverently, "Our temple is sacred. It is the holiest place in all of Jerusalem. We come here to worship and give praise to the Lord for the many blessings He has bestowed on us." Benjamin had believed his father's words. There was no reason to doubt them.

Inside the temple area, Benjamin ended up in the middle of a group of men. He looked for his father and grandfather, but he couldn't find them anywhere. The women and their daughters watched from the Women's Court. He wondered if Rachel could see him.

Daniel squeezed in next to him and began to utter a prayer. Benjamin nudged him with an elbow. "Shalom," he whispered.

Daniel nodded, his chubby face scrunched into a grin.

A High Priest, dressed in a white robe with a red sash cinched around his waist, sprinkled the altar with a blood offering. Benjamin's empty stomach growled and felt queasy. Father stepped forward out of the assembly and lit the altar's incense.

The High Priest recited the Aaronic blessing: "The Lord bless you, and keep you. The Lord make His face shine on you, and be gracious to you. The Lord lift up His countenance on you, and give you peace."

The Torah was carried in and handed to Father. He

held it as the High Priest unrolled the scroll and read the words of the Ten Commandments.

During the reading, a stranger came and stood by Benjamin. He was tall in stature. His long dark hair fell to his shoulders. The brown robe he wore seemed quite ordinary, but it smelled of cedar. Where had this man come from?

Curiosity got the best of Benjamin and he inched toward the man. He got so close that the stranger's robe brushed his arm. A tremendous wave of heat washed through his body. He began to tremble, and his knees went weak. What was happening? Overwhelmed by a wonderful and weird sensation that flooded his body, he could hardly catch his breath.

The man smiled at him. His dark brown eyes reminded Benjamin of his mother's. He stared at them. Realizing what he was doing, he glanced away.

His breath was still coming in short, quick gasps, but he finally stopped shaking. He was determined to sneak another look.

The stranger's weathered hands appeared rough, as those of a hard laborer. The short beard was cut to show he was still single. What was it about him that made Benjamin feel so odd?

The Levite choir began to sing. The man joined in. His voice, strong and soothing, enticed Benjamin to open his mouth and burst into song. But the sound that came out was high-pitched and squeaky. His voice was changing, but why did it have to crack now?

Feeling self-conscious, he quit singing and closed his eyes. He listened to the pleasant sounding voice of the stranger. A calm sensation flowed through him. He had never experienced anything like it before, and he wanted it to last.

The Levite choir finished their last song, and Benjamin opened his eyes. The stranger was leaving. He crossed over to the Nicanor Gate and paused for a moment before he slipped through to the outer courtyard.

Without hesitation, Benjamin went after him. Halfway across the courtyard, he realized that the service had not ended. Still, he was drawn to follow the man.

Outside, he glanced around. Some stragglers were still near the booths of the moneychangers and the merchants. The man in the brown robe was nowhere to be seen.

Then, men and their sons began to file out through the gate. The service must have ended.

Daniel ran over to Benjamin. "Why did you leave? Your father's not going to be pleased with you."

"Not so loud," Benjamin said, putting his finger to his lips. "I snuck out to find the stranger who stood next to me, but I don't know where he went."

Daniel frowned. "That man is the rabbi everyone's talking about."

"You know him?"

"My father constantly speaks of him and says he

wants nothing to do with this new rabbi, Jesus," Daniel said, folding his hands across his chest.

Benjamin raised an eyebrow. "His name is Jesus?"

"That's what he's called. My father thinks that he's a threat to our way of life. He does things that no other rabbi would do."

"Like what?"

Daniel shrugged. "How should I know? My father told me to stay away from him. You should too."

"I can't help myself. There's something unusual about this Jesus. I don't know what it is, but he's different – very different."

Daniel jabbed a finger at Benjamin. "You'd better ignore him like I'm doing if you're going to be a rabbi."

He pushed his friend's hand away. "Maybe I won't become one."

"What? We made a pact to become rabbis together. You can't break it. If you do, what will I do?"

A loud crash sounded nearby. "What was that?" Daniel asked.

Benjamin turned toward the noise. "Let's find out." They pushed their way through the crowded outer courtyard to where a group of people had gathered.

The stranger was knocking over the moneychangers' tables. Coins flew in every direction and clinked as they hit the cobblestones. Children scrambled to snatch them up.

Jesus shouted, "God's house is a place of prayer. You are making it into a den of thieves."

"Listen to him," Daniel said. "Jesus is a trouble-maker, just like my father said. He talks as if he knows what God wants."

"Selling sacrificial animals for a profit always seemed wrong to me," Benjamin said under his breath.

A crowd surrounded Jesus. A man wearing a Pharisee's headpiece yelled, "Who do you think you are to demand the moneychangers leave? You're the one who doesn't belong here."

Before Benjamin could hear Jesus' reply, his father seized his arm. "I have been looking for you. We do not want to be part of this rebellion."

He couldn't believe what his father was saying. "Where's Grandfather?" he asked, looking around.

"I told him to go on ahead. We are leaving right now." Father let go of Benjamin's arm.

"Daniel, meet me by the dogwood tree before evening prayer. I have something important to tell you," Benjamin whispered hurriedly before he followed after his father.

SIX

THE MEETING PLACE

Benjamin didn't want to leave, but he had to obey his father. He glanced over his shoulder for a last look at Jesus, but people were still gathered around him. What was his father afraid of? And why did he insist on leaving?

When they approached the North Gate, the soldier, Marcus, was leaning against the limestone wall.

As Benjamin and Father passed in front of him, Marcus stepped out and blocked their path. "Rabbi, where are you going in such a hurry?"

"We are going home," Father said, staring at the ground.

"Where are you coming from?" Marcus demanded, his hand resting on the handle of his sword.

"From the temple."

"Ah, yes, the temple. I know all about your holy rituals and your one God. Do you think your God can protect you from me and all the gods I serve?"

Father didn't answer.

But to Benjamin's surprise, he heard his own voice, loud and clear, say, "We've committed no crime. We're going home, it's late."

Marcus' eyes narrowed. "I remember you. You're that stubborn pack mule who carried my gear, and now you dare to tell me what to do?"

"We have a right to leave the city," Benjamin said, again surprised at his own boldness.

"You Jews are a nuisance. Will you never learn that we Romans control Jerusalem?" He shoved Benjamin aside. "Go home. I'll deal with you later when I have more time." Marcus left and headed in the direction of the Antonia Fortress.

"You carried that soldier's gear?" Father asked, frowning.

Benjamin nodded.

His father shook his head. "They treat us however they please. I am sorry you have to put up with them. One day it will be different, you will see. Let us be on our way. Your grandfather will worry if we're not home soon."

"Father, why didn't you speak up to the soldier?"

"I learned long ago that to answer back makes them strike out in anger. It is better to say nothing."

Benjamin nodded again, remembering the sting of the soldier's sword on his ankle. As they left the city in silence, he wanted to ask his father if he was afraid of the soldier, but he didn't know how to do it without sounding disrespectful.

At the house, his father faced him. "Do not judge me too harshly. Getting involved in the rebellion or speaking out against Roman authority can put us in grave danger. If they think we are being insolent and causing problems, they will never leave us in peace." He turned and went into the house.

Benjamin knew that what his father spoke was true. But how much abuse were they going to take before they struck back?

Inside, Grandfather was placing a plate of fish and figs on the table next to some bread. "Where have you been? I was concerned."

"A soldier stopped us," Benjamin said as he stood by his place at the table.

"The one at the North Gate? The one with the scar?"

"Yes, but let us not talk about him during dinner," Father said. "We do not want to spoil our meal." He lifted his hands in prayer. "Lord our God, we thank you for..."

Benjamin's mind wandered to when his mother said the dinner prayers with great reverence. He missed hearing her voice.

As he came out of his daze, he heard his father asking for God's blessing on each one of them and on the food. Then they sat down and ate in silence. When Mother was alive, dinnertime was filled with laughter and talk of the day's events. Would that kind of happiness ever fill their house again?

In a hurry to meet Daniel, Benjamin helped himself

to a piece of bread and smothered it with honey. Taking big bites, he swallowed, barely chewing.

"Slow down," Grandfather said, smiling. "We don't want you choking. There's plenty of time and plenty of food."

Benjamin grinned, still shoving bread into his mouth.

Father remained quiet and lost in thought.

At the end of the meal, Grandfather stretched. "I'm going to take a walk through the olive grove before bed. Would you like to join me, Samuel?"

Father leaned back from the table. "Maybe another time, Jacob. I am tired. It has been a long day."

"I'm meeting Daniel by the dogwood tree. May I leave?"

"Once everything is put away," Father said.

While clearing the table, Benjamin recalled how, at the end of each meal, Father would spend time teaching him stories from the Torah. Now he just sat at the table and read by himself.

"I'm finished. Is it alright if I leave?"

His father nodded, but didn't look up.

Benjamin ran out of the house and through the olive grove. A slight breeze rustled the leaves. He reached the dogwood tree, leaned his back against the rough bark, and breathed deeply. The air smelled like the fragrant perfume his mother always wore. He glanced around, expecting to see her, but of course, she wasn't there.

He tried to picture her face. It was taking longer and longer to see her clearly. He sighed and looked up into the sky. The sun hung low in the west, and the moon was overhead.

"Sorry I'm late," Daniel called as he came down the path. "Rachel insisted on coming along. You know how girls are. They'll fuss until their headscarf is just right."

Benjamin's mind went to the baby who died with his mother. "Be glad you have a sister," he said. "She's a blessing and don't you forget it."

"You don't have to get angry. I only—"

"Daniel's just being Daniel," Rachel interrupted, as she came and stood next to Benjamin. Her almond-shaped eyes caught the reflection of the moon. He swallowed hard. It was only a few years ago that she was the little girl who constantly pestered them, begging to play in their games. During this past year, Rachel kept to herself. It seemed as if overnight she had grown as tall and as slender as a willow.

"What's so important that it can't wait until tomorrow?" Daniel asked, tugging at the neck of his tunic.

"An odd thing happened during service today. The new rabbi's cloak brushed against me, and I felt heat travel through my whole body. I started to shake, and my knees went weak. I wasn't afraid of him or anything. It's just that I wasn't sure what was going on. His eyes reminded me of my mother's – they looked so kind and gentle. I felt a peace I've never experienced before."

"That's crazy," Daniel said.

"I don't understand it myself, but I know what I felt."

Rachel smiled. "I wish I could have stood next to him."

"Men don't pray next to women at service."

"Jesus would," Benjamin said, wanting to defend Rachel.

"That's the problem with Jesus. My father says he does whatever he pleases."

"Tell me, what happened after I left the courtyard?" Benjamin asked, not wanting to argue with Daniel about Jesus.

"The temple guards drove the crowd away, and Jesus disappeared. Why did your father insist on leaving?"

"He said he didn't want to be involved."

"I can understand why." Daniel started to pace.

"What's the matter with you, Daniel? Why are you so upset?"

"My father's been irritable ever since Jesus came to Jerusalem. I think it has rubbed off on me. Sorry."

Benjamin wanted to laugh, but he knew Daniel was serious. Rachel leaned in close to him and lowered her voice, "I overheard my father telling one of the temple priests that they're concerned about Jesus because he healed a lame man on the Sabbath. Jesus told the man to pick up his mat and walk, and the man did. My father insists that some people believe Jesus is the Messiah. Others think he's a false prophet who is deceiving everyone. What do you think, Benjamin?"

He felt her breath on his face and gulped down the lump in his throat. But then he quickly gathered his thoughts and said, "I think that if Jesus heals the sick, he must have amazing powers. To say he's the one promised for us, I don't know. I don't believe God will ever send us the Messiah."

Rachel's dark eyes grew wide. "What do you think about him healing on the Sabbath? Do you think it's wrong?"

"If someone receives a healing, it can't be wrong, no matter when it happens."

"It's against the law," Daniel's voice cut in. He stopped pacing. "We must follow the law as it's written. There are a lot of false prophets who claim to be healers."

"You sound just like our father," Rachel said.

"Maybe I do! We have to go now, it's time for evening prayers. Father and Mother will wonder where we are." Daniel headed across the olive grove. "Are you coming, Rachel?"

"Go ahead, Daniel," Benjamin shouted after him. "Leave if you want to. See if I care."

"You'll have to forgive Daniel. He hasn't been himself lately. Like my father, the stories people are passing around about Jesus make him nervous."

"You'd better leave, too, Rachel. I don't want you getting into trouble if you're late for prayer."

"What about you? Won't your father wonder where you are?"

"It doesn't matter. I'll go in soon."

"Shalom, Benjamin."

"Shalom, Rachel." He watched her until she was out of sight. All the while remembering what she had said about Jesus.

"The sky has turned pink. We should have nice

weather tomorrow." Grandfather's voice came from behind him.

"You startled me," Benjamin said, turning quickly.

"I'm sorry. You did seem deep in thought."

"I was thinking about the new rabbi, Jesus. Have you heard any stories about him?"

"Only that the High Council is suspicious about what he's preaching. They say the healing he's doing is not according to our laws."

"Do you think that's true?"

Grandfather stroked his beard. "It seems to me that the man is doing God's work."

"Do you really think it's God's work?"

"I do." Grandfather started to walk down the path toward the house.

Benjamin fell in step next to him. "Why does Jesus heal on the Sabbath?"

"I'm not sure. He doesn't seem to care what day it is when he cures the sick."

"Rachel said she overheard her father saying that some people think Jesus is the Messiah."

"I admire what the man is doing, but I hardly think he's the Messiah. The Messiah will not come to heal people. He'll be a great warrior, one who will lead our people in battle and free us from the tyranny of Rome."

Before they entered the house, the bright pink of the sky turned a deep purple. The olive trees, nearly hiding the moon, cast dark shadows over the land.

SEVEN

THE DREAM

Benjamin lay in bed, his mind filled with thoughts of Jesus. He closed his eyes and drifted off to sleep. A dream formed wherein Jesus stood next to Mother's deathbed…

Jesus placed his hand on her wounded side. At once, Mother's pale cheeks became rosy. Her eyes opened and sparkled with new life. She laughed, and Father heard her and came running into the room. He knelt by her bed. They embraced. But then, the figure of Jesus faded and a black cloud moved in. It hovered over their house. Thunder rumbled in the distance, and a bolt of lightning shot out of the menacing sky. It struck the thatched roof, engulfing the home in flames. The blaze burned brightly, consuming Benjamin's parents.

Benjamin bolted upright out of his sleep, his heart beat wildly. He expected to be swallowed up by the fire, but only darkness surrounded him. He realized he had only been dreaming.

Benjamin bit down on his lip. If Jesus had been in Jerusalem during the uprising, he could have made a difference. Maybe he could have healed Mother. Rubbing his eyes, Benjamin swallowed hard. Lying back down, he stared into the dark until finally he returned to an uneasy sleep.

Before dawn, he awoke to loud snores. They came from Grandfather, who slept on a cot across the room. Tired, but too restless to stay in bed, Benjamin threw back his cover, grabbed his tunic and a small leather money pouch, and crept into the outer room to dress. After doing so, he hung the pouch around his neck and the coins inside clinked together. He strapped on his sandals, and went outside.

The grass was damp from the night's rain. He was convinced the thunder and lightning of his dream had been real. Frightened by the thought of the fire, he wondered if bad dreams ever came true. Fear followed him as he hurried to the olive grove.

At the dogwood tree, he sat and watched the sun creep above the horizon. He closed his eyes, trying to recall the dream of Jesus healing his mother. As a picture began to form, he slipped back into sleep. Suddenly, a loud bray pierced the air, startling him awake. Trudging up the road into Jerusalem, an old man led a donkey laden with bundles of sticks.

In a field across the road, a group of men gathered near a fig tree. The only one Benjamin recognized was Jesus, who was talking to the other men. It was hard to hear what he was saying, so Benjamin snuck over and hid behind the dense branches of a broom bush.

Jesus reached to pick a fig, but there was no fruit on the tree. "You may never bear fruit again," he said. In that instant, the tree dried up, and all the leaves fell to the ground. Benjamin rubbed his eyes in disbelief.

A bushy-bearded man scratched his head. "Master, how did you do that?"

Jesus laughed. "The truth is, Peter, if you have faith and trust, you, too, can do what I did. You can even speak to a mountain saying, 'Be tossed into the sea,' and it will be done."

Another man standing nearby wrung his hands. "What do you mean? I don't understand."

"Thomas, if you have faith, you will receive all you ask for in prayer."

Benjamin shook his head. How could he believe Jesus? His urgent prayer for his mother hadn't been answered.

Jesus walked over to the bush where Benjamin was hiding and knelt beside him. "Benjamin, our prayers are not always answered in the way we expect."

Had Jesus read his thoughts? His heart was pounding so hard, he felt as though it would burst right out of his tunic.

Jesus continued, "If you believe, then all things are possible. I have had my eye on you from the very beginning." He smiled, got up, and made his way to the road that led up to Jerusalem. He motioned to his companions, and they followed.

Jesus had his eye on him? What did that mean? Benjamin was puzzled. Leaping to his feet, he watched the group until they disappeared through the North Gate. He wanted to go too, but his father would be angry if he went. Still, he couldn't resist. This was too important. He ran up the road as fast as he could, trying not to think of the consequences.

He was out of breath when he entered the city's gate. Inside the limestone wall, he searched the crowds for Jesus and his followers, but they were nowhere in sight. The sun was furiously hot. Sweat trickled down Benjamin's back as he wandered into the marketplace where noisy bargain hunters bartered to get the best deal. The mouthwatering smells of spices and honey that drifted over from the food booths made his stomach growl.

He stopped at a booth stacked high with persimmons and remembered jumping over them during the uprising. He wanted to walk away, but the lure of the red fruit and his hunger pains were too powerful to ignore.

From experience, he knew that the reddest persimmon with the most wrinkles would be the juiciest. Examining a few, he picked the finest one. He dug a coin from the pouch around his neck and placed it in the vendor's coarse hand.

A large, overturned clay pot near a date stand looked

like a good place to sit. He plunked down, stripped the fruit, and tossed the peels to the ground. With the first bite, juice trickled from the corner of his mouth. He wiped it away with his sleeve.

At the next booth, a young woman carrying a baby on her hip purchased olive oil. She reminded him of his mother and he sighed deeply.

Out of nowhere, a small, scrawny boy stepped in front of Benjamin and blocked his view. The youth's hair had twigs tangled in it, and his face was streaked with sweat and dirt. The tunic he wore was tattered and torn. If Mother were still alive, Benjamin thought she would take that young stray home, clean him up, and give him a decent meal.

The boy crept over to the date stand, which was stacked high with the dark fruit. The minute the vendor turned his back to wait on a customer, the boy snatched a handful of the plump dates. The vendor was faster. He seized the boy's skinny arm yelling, "Thief!"

Without hesitation, Benjamin jumped up. "Let him go! I'll pay."

The merchant, still gripping the boy's arm with one hand, shoved the other one in Benjamin's face. "Give me the money first. Then, I'll turn him loose."

Benjamin pulled a coin from his pouch and dropped it into the outstretched hand. He smiled to himself as he realized that this was just what his mother would have done. The vendor released the boy, and the child, still clutching the dates, darted off into the crowd.

Benjamin wanted to go after him, but over the din of the marketplace, he heard someone calling his name.

"Benjamin! Benjamin!" Rachel ran up to him and grabbed his arm. Her cheeks were rosy, and she gasped for breath. "Come quick! Some bullies are beating up Daniel."

Without asking any questions, Benjamin raced with her down a side street to the end of a narrow passageway. Daniel was on the ground, struggling beneath two large boys. They were punching his face and trying to rip the pouch from around his neck. Daniel was doing his best to fight them off.

"Leave him alone," Benjamin shouted. He pulled one of the bullies off Daniel and wrestled him to the ground. The boy squirmed from Benjamin's grasp and hopped up with his fists swinging.

"Look out!" Rachel called. Benjamin, getting to his feet, ducked. The boy, losing his balance, missed. A quick shove from Benjamin and the bully toppled to the ground. Looking surprised, he scrambled up and scurried down the nearest alley. The other ruffian, seeing that his friend had left, leapt off Daniel and darted away.

"Cowards!" Benjamin yelled. Then he glanced at Daniel. "Your lip is bleeding, and your eye is puffy."

"I could've taken them if they'd come at me one at a time."

"You could have," Benjamin agreed as he extended his friend a hand.

Daniel grinned and took it.

Rachel pulled a small white cloth from her sleeve. "Here, let me wipe your lip."

"I'm all right." Daniel brushed her hand aside and licked off the blood.

"Why did they attack you?" Benjamin asked.

"They wanted my money. They must have seen me buying honey cakes."

"Daniel's pouch always bulges with coins for sweets."

Her brother jiggled the leather bag that hung around his neck. "Yes, but they didn't get any money. Nor did they get any honey cakes, since I'd already eaten them."

Benjamin laughed and shook his head. "No wonder those ruffians tried to rob you. Rachel, how did you know where to find me?"

"We saw you sitting by the date booth. Daniel was still angry because of what you said about Jesus last night, so he hurried me off in the opposite direction. When those bullies pounced on him, he yelled at me to find you."

"Thanks for coming," Daniel said sheepishly.

"You'd do the same for me. Let's get out of here. If those ruffians are desperate for money, they might come back with some of their friends."

The three hurried back to the marketplace where a crowd had gathered by the Market Hall.

"Let's find out what's going on," Benjamin said, edging forward. They worked their way into the crowd.

Jesus and some of his companions were standing in the middle of it.

A Pharisee, dressed in a blue robe, was speaking loudly, "Jesus, we know you are an honest man. You are not fooled by false teachings. You teach according to God's laws, so I ask you, is it right to pay taxes to Caesar?"

Benjamin wiggled between two men to get a closer look.

"Why do you try to trap me?" Jesus asked. He motioned to the Pharisees. "Show me the coin that pays the census tax."

The man tossed him one.

Jesus caught it and held it up to the crowd. "Whose picture is on this coin?"

"Caesar's!" the people shouted.

"There is your answer. Give to Caesar what is Caesar's, and give to God what is God's."

"What's he talking about?" Daniel frowned. "Some of our money must go for the temple's taxes."

"You don't understand," Benjamin replied. "He used a Roman coin, not a Jewish shekel."

"That's right!" Rachel said, nodding.

Jesus tossed the coin back and walked away as the crowd followed.

"Come on," Benjamin said, gesturing. "Let's not lose sight of him."

As people surrounded Jesus again, a man wearing the long flowing robe of a Sadducee approached him.

"Of all the commandments, which one is the most important?" he asked.

Jesus looked into the sky. "Hear this, O Israel. Serve one God. There is no other. First, you are to love the Lord your God with all your heart, soul, mind, and strength. Secondly, you are to love your neighbor as yourself. There are no other commandments greater than these."

"Well said, Teacher," the Sadducee replied. "God is one and there is no other but him. To love him with all your heart and with all your strength is worth more than all the burnt offerings and sacrifices made at the temple."

"Did you hear that?" Daniel said loudly. "That man says our temple offerings are worthless."

"Keep your voice down," Rachel whispered, tugging at Daniel's sleeve. "People are staring at us."

"I don't care!" Daniel said, pulling away.

Benjamin ignored Daniel. He couldn't help wondering about Jesus' words. 'Love God and love your neighbor as yourself.' That was hard to do since God didn't care about him. His neighbors were the Pharisees, Sadducees, and Romans, and they were impossible to love. And if Jesus was the Messiah, why was he talking about love instead of driving the Romans out of Jerusalem?

Rachel nudged Benjamin. "Look, there's your father."

Out of the crowd, his father emerged and stopped in

front of them. "What are you doing here? You should be home working with your grandfather."

"I'm sorry, I had to—"

"To what, disobey? I told you to stay away from that man." Father took hold of his arm. "Come home with me at once!"

Benjamin's face burned with embarrassment. Why was his father treating him like a child?

"And you two," Father said, looking at Daniel and Rachel, "do your parents know you are here?"

"No, Rabbi Samuel," Daniel and Rachel said together, looking at the ground.

"You had better get home too."

"Yes, Rabbi Samuel," they said in unison.

"Come, son. Your grandfather will be waiting for us."

Benjamin hung his head and left with his father. He had no other choice but to obey.

EIGHT

UNCLE SOLOMON AND AUNT ESTHER

Early the next morning, Benjamin straddled a large limb of an olive tree. Still angry about being treated like a child in front of Rachel, he made quick work of sawing off the dead branches. Didn't his father realize he was a man?

"It's your turn to get water," Grandfather called from below. "Did you forget?"

"Sorry, I'll fetch it right away."

Benjamin scrambled down and dropped the shearing knife next to the tree. He dashed across the grove and sprinted past the dogwood tree. He stopped suddenly. Loud shouts resonated from a hillside on the far side of the road. "Hosanna! Hosanna! Blessed is the name of the Lord! Hosanna!"

A large crowd was winding its way down a narrow path that ended at the road into the city. They were shouting praises to a man who was riding on a donkey.

As they got closer, he recognized the man. It was the rabbi, Jesus. People were waving palm branches in the air. "Hosanna! Blessed is the King of Israel." Their voices grew louder.

Watching the crowd pass, Benjamin decided to follow them to the gate, but no farther. He didn't want his father upset with him again. He stayed a distance behind the cheering crowd.

Arriving at the North Gate, the people threw their cloaks on the ground in front of the donkey. They continued to wave the palm branches in the air and shout, "Hosanna! Hosanna!"

Jesus rode into the city under a canopy of palms.

Why were they calling Jesus a king? He wasn't a king. He was a rabbi, a teacher.

Standing near a cedar tree outside the North Gate, Benjamin tried to figure out what had just happened.

Daniel and Rachel strolled out of the gate. Had they seen Jesus enter? Did they know what was going on? He ran to meet them.

"Did you see Jesus riding a donkey and surrounded by people shouting praises to him? What was going on?"

"We saw him." Rachel's face was flushed and glowing. "The people were tossing their cloaks down in front of him like royalty."

"What a spectacle!" Daniel's face scrunched up in disgust. "They were parading him like he was a king."

"Do you have any idea why?"

"No, and I don't care. If you ask me, they're acting like fools," Daniel said.

Rachel shifted the small basket of pears she carried. "I'll find out for you. My father's at a meeting in the city. He's sure to know."

"What meeting?" Benjamin asked.

"This morning my father told my mother that the elders requested a meeting to talk about Jesus."

"Will you meet me at the dogwood tree this evening and tell me what you find out?"

"I'll be there."

"She can't come. She's not allowed to go out alone in the evening."

Benjamin put a hand on Daniel's shoulder. "Will you come with her?"

Daniel shrugged free from Benjamin's hand. "All right, I'll come, even though I have no interest in what's going on."

"It's agreed. I'll see you both tonight."

"Let's go, Rachel. I'm hungry and thirsty."

"Oh no, I forgot. I'm supposed to get water for Grandfather."

Benjamin took off running. At the cistern, he picked up the clay waterpot that was tied with a piece of rope. He lowered it into the opening. Once it was filled, he pulled it up and set it on the ground.

"Benjamin, my dear boy," a familiar voice called from behind him.

It was Aunt Esther, his mother's sister. She was the

only one who called him "dear boy." As he turned, his aunt wrapped him into her ample arms and kissed his cheeks. She kept holding him and wouldn't let go. The fuss and attention made him smile. Aunt Esther not only looked like his mother, she smelled of the same perfume. He felt wonderful and hoped it wouldn't end.

Uncle Solomon was standing next to a wooden cart, holding the reins of a donkey. His bald head glistened with sweat. His bushy brows arched over his eyes like giant caterpillars. A full gray beard ended at his portly belly.

Aunt Esther finally loosened her embrace. She held him at arm's length. Her headscarf had slipped back. It showed a part of her gray hair that was wound tightly in a thick braid around the crown of her head. Her dark eyes widened. "Are you all right, dear boy?"

"Yes, now that you're here."

"How about a big hug for your old uncle?" Uncle Solomon opened his hefty arms and pulled Benjamin into a bear hug. Patting his nephew on the back, he said, "You've grown. I used to tower over you, now I'm the one who has to look up."

Feeling a mile high, Benjamin grinned. "I'm glad you're here, Uncle, but you're early. It's not Passover yet."

"A caravan was leaving Tiberias. We didn't want to travel alone so we came with them, and your aunt couldn't wait to get here. She wants to cook you some decent meals. She's certain none of you are getting properly fed." Uncle Solomon rubbed his belly.

By now, Benjamin was grinning so hard, his face hurt. "Auntie, I can't wait to get a taste of your freshly baked bread."

"Dear, dear boy. You remind me so much of your mother." She started to cry.

"Now, now." Uncle Solomon put his arm around her shoulders. "You promised me you wouldn't shed any tears in front of the boy."

"I can't help it."

Benjamin was choking back his own tears.

Aunt Esther dabbed her eyes with her sleeve.

Uncle Solomon kept his arm around her. "Benjamin, is your father home? And where's your grandfather?"

"Father's at the house and Grandfather's in the olive grove. He's waiting for me to get water. I'm sure he's wondering what's taking so long."

"Go quickly," Aunt Esther said, continuing to wipe her eyes. "Tell him we've arrived. We'll go and find your father."

As soon as they left, Benjamin untied the pot, and holding it by the handles, he raced off toward the olive grove. Water sloshed down the front of his tunic. "Grandfather, Grandfather! Uncle Solomon and Aunt Esther are here for Passover!"

NINE

THE MAN FROM GALILEE

Benjamin hovered near his aunt, inhaling the delicious smells from the pot of soup that simmered on top of the clay oven, and the fresh bread that baked inside.

Aunt Esther spread a white cloth on the long wooden table. In the middle of it, she placed empty soup bowls, a large bowl of wild wheat salad, a jar of honey, a pitcher of goat's milk, and a jug of wine that Uncle Solomon had brought from Tiberias.

"Will we eat soon?" Benjamin asked.

"Do not rush your aunt," Father said. He stood near the table, talking with Grandfather and Uncle Solomon.

Aunt Esther held out a large crock of hot soup. "Dear boy, give me a hand."

Benjamin took it and placed it on the table. Some broth sloshed over the sides onto the white cloth. "Sorry, Auntie," he said, his face flushing red.

She handed him a rag. "That's all right. Just don't burn yourself."

He quickly wiped the spill. Then Aunt Esther brought a loaf of warm bread wrapped in a cloth, and set it on the table.

Benjamin dropped down on a floor cushion, ready to eat.

Father arched his brow. "Your aunt's fine meal deserves a blessing."

Benjamin jumped up quickly.

Father held his hands over the food and prayed, "Lord God, we thank you for the safe arrival of Solomon and Esther. For the abundant supply of food that has been set before us, we give you praise. May we always recognize that everything we have comes directly from your generosity."

This time Benjamin waited until everyone was seated before he plopped down. Father ladled soup into bowls and passed them around. Benjamin sipped the hot broth, savoring each mouthful. A small dish of wild wheat salad was placed before him. He scooped a large portion into his mouth.

Father frowned. "Benjamin, where are your manners?"

Aunt Esther winked and handed her nephew the loaf of warm bread. He tore off a large chunk and passed the rest to Grandfather. He smeared his piece with honey.

As he bit into the sweet syrup, it squished through his teeth. Aunt Esther poured him a cup of goat's milk. He gulped it down, barely taking a breath.

The only time Grandfather and Uncle Solomon looked up from their plates was to tear off another piece of bread. Once the meal was over, Father poured the adults a cup of wine. "Tell us, Solomon, how are your sons?" he asked.

"Reuben and Asher are at the Sea of Galilee tending to the fishing boat in our absence."

"Isaac is busy with his rabbinical studies," Aunt Esther added proudly, "and he tends to the fruit trees."

"My son will continue his studies after he finishes helping in the olive grove," Father said. Then he sipped a bit of wine.

Benjamin slumped to avoid his father's eyes. He didn't have the courage to tell him that he no longer wanted to become a rabbi. He glanced at Grandfather, wondering if he would say anything about it.

But Grandfather didn't even look at him. He was busy brushing bread crumbs from his beard. "Is Reuben betrothed yet?" he asked. "Will we be invited to Tiberias for a wedding soon?"

Aunt Esther shook her head. "No, no, Reuben's not ready for marriage. None of the boys are ready to leave home."

"It's her cooking they won't leave." Uncle Solomon laughed. Then clearing his throat, he asked, "Have you heard about the rabbi, the Nazarene who preached in Tiberias and around the Galilean countryside?"

Benjamin straightened up. "The Nazarene? Who are you talking about, Uncle?"

"Jesus. I hear he's in Jerusalem."

Father set down his wine cup. "We have heard and seen him."

Uncle Solomon leaned forward and lowered his voice as if he was afraid of being overheard. "Many claim that Jesus will lead a Jewish army against the Romans."

"Uncle, I thought the Jews were waiting for the Messiah to do that."

"Some think Jesus is the Messiah."

"I knew he was different," Benjamin said, more to himself than anyone.

Father rubbed his finger around the top of the wine cup. "Many stories are told about this man."

Aunt Esther smoothed her apron. "In Cana, they say Jesus attended a wedding with his mother. When the host ran out of wine Jesus instructed the servers to take some empty jars, fill them with water, and bring them to him. He told them to taste it and the water had turned into wine."

"That's impossible!" Grandfather said his eyes wide.

"I don't know, Jacob." Uncle Solomon shrugged. "They say he also heals the sick. The latest story is he raised his friend Lazarus from the dead."

"Unbelievable!"

"It's said that Jesus came to Lazarus' tomb and wept. When he called, 'Lazarus, come forth.' Out of the tomb came the man bound hand and foot in his burial cloth. He had been in the tomb for four days. What do you think about that, Samuel?"

Father fingered the top of his wine cup again. "This morning in the market, I saw a man I know who has been paralyzed since birth, but he was walking. He eagerly told me that Jesus instructed him to pick up his mat and walk, and without hesitation, he obeyed. If I had not known the man personally, I would not have believed him."

Benjamin stared at his father. Had he changed his mind about Jesus? Did he now understand that Jesus was different from the other rabbis?

Father picked up the wine jug, refilling everyone's cups as he continued, "Many elders at the temple speak harshly about Jesus. They say they will not allow him to keep healing the sick. They believe his practices are unholy, and they will not rest until they stop him. I know meetings are being held, but I steer clear of them. To get involved is dangerous."

Benjamin slumped back on the cushion. Why was his father still afraid to take a stand? And what did he really think of Jesus? Benjamin had to know. He drew in a breath. "Father, do you believe Jesus is the Messiah?"

His father hesitated a moment before saying, "Son, I know the man is healing people. But is he the Messiah? I cannot say."

"Father, if Jesus is doing such great things, why is he feared?"

"The Pharisees and Sadducees are threatened because many from their congregations believe Jesus when he speaks about the coming of a new Kingdom. They are afraid of losing their power over the people."

"Why do the Romans hate him?"

"Because he has gained such a large following

among the poor, they fear more and more people will be involved in uprisings. They are afraid there will be a war."

A long silence ensued. Finally, Grandfather stretched and yawned. "Our relatives have traveled a far distance. They are tired and need sleep. We can talk tomorrow."

Uncle Solomon got up from the table. "Yes, the journey was demanding. I'll say goodnight. Esther, don't be long. You must be tired too."

Grandfather retired into the bedroom he shared with Benjamin. Uncle Solomon disappeared into Father's bedroom where he and Aunt Esther would sleep. Benjamin and Father helped Aunt Esther clear the table. Jesus was not mentioned again. Although he wanted to hear more, it would have to wait.

It was late. In the dark of his room, Benjamin crawled into bed fully clothed. He rubbed his eyes, determined to stay awake to join Daniel and Rachel at the dogwood tree. He was certain that Rachel would have news of why the people were treating Jesus like a king.

He listened while his father said his evening prayers quietly. After Father finished, he came into the bedroom and slipped into a cot next to Grandfather, who was already snoring. Loud snores penetrated the thin wall from Father's bedroom where Uncle Solomon and Aunt Esther slept.

Soon the heavy breathing in the house convinced Benjamin that everyone was asleep. He wrapped a cloak around his shoulders and slipped out of the house. The evening air blew cold as he hurried down the path in the dark.

The trees swaying in the wind took on the form of lions ready to pounce. Overhead, branches hung down like slithering snakes. A chill slid down Benjamin's back, and he made a dash for the dogwood tree.

"Is that you, Benjamin?" Rachel stepped out of the shadows and touched his hand. Her hand was cold.

"We've been waiting a long time." Daniel sounded upset.

"I'm sorry. My aunt and uncle arrived from Tiberias and we stayed up late talking. I had to wait until everyone was asleep."

Rachel twisted a small white cloth in her fingers and glanced nervously from side to side.

Benjamin lowered his voice, "Did you find out why they were treating Jesus like a king?"

"No, she didn't," Daniel said, shaking his head. "But we did overhear our parents talking after our father returned from the meeting in the city. The Sanhedrin Council has a plan to get rid of Jesus. Our father is frantic about it, because he witnessed one of Jesus' miracle healings today and with the other stories he's heard recently, he's convinced that the rabbi is the Messiah after all. But I don't know..."

Benjamin heard confusion in his friend's voice because of Rabbi Aaron's sudden change of heart.

"Are you alright, Daniel?" he asked.

"I'm not sure. I wish I had been with my father when he saw the healing." He paused a moment, and then said, "Rachel, we should leave. If Father finds us gone, he'll worry."

"You'd better go," Benjamin said reluctantly.

Rachel shook her head. "Not until I tell you what else our parents were talking about." Her voice dropped to a whisper. "The leaders of the Sanhedrin Council are going to arrest Jesus. They have become fearful since he brought his friend Lazarus back from the dead. They're afraid this has convinced the people he is truly the Messiah."

"I don't understand. The Messiah will lead us in battle against the Romans. Jesus is a holy man. He heals and preaches love."

"There's talk of a trial," Rachel said.

"A trial? What laws has he broken?"

Rachel leaned closer. "The council will ask the governor, Pilate, to convict Jesus by using Roman laws, not by the laws of our people. That's what I overheard my father say."

"Rachel, it's not safe to talk about this." Daniel took hold of his sister's arm. "We must leave, now."

"Shalom, Benjamin," Rachel called as she and Daniel hurried down the path.

"Shalom, Rachel. Shalom, Daniel," Benjamin called after them as he watched them disappear into the darkness.

He made his way back to the house, all the while thinking about what Rachel had told him. How could the Sanhedrin Council condemn an innocent man like Jesus, but if they did, would there be justice for anyone?

TEN

THE SEDER MEAL

The next morning, even with the covers pulled over his head, Benjamin couldn't block out Father's firm voice in the outer room. "If we do not reach the market early, the best lambs will be taken."

"Make sure you pick a small one," Aunt Esther said. "The big ones have too much gristle and are hard to chew."

The customary ritual for Passover included purchasing a year-old lamb for the Seder meal. This morning the men were going to the marketplace to select it.

In previous years, Benjamin had stayed home with his mother to prepare the house for the festivities. This year, since turning thirteen, he would go along with the men.

His father called from the other room, "Son, are you awake? Get dressed. We are ready to leave."

Benjamin had always eagerly anticipated the Seder meal, and the retelling of the Israelites' flight from slavery intrigued him. With the death of his mother still fresh in his mind, he felt sick at the thought of partaking in the killing of a lamb.

Aunt Esther came and stood in the bedroom door. "Hurry. They're leaving without you."

Tossing back his cover, he leaped up, pulled on his tunic, and dashed to the front door. Once there, he jumped from one foot to the other while strapping on his sandals. Aunt Esther was holding a piece of honey-smothered bread. "Take this. I don't want you to go hungry."

"Don't worry, Auntie. With your fresh bread each day, I'm getting as fat as an ox." He kissed her cheek and grabbed the sticky delight. He ate it as he ran out of the house, through the olive grove, and up the road.

After he caught up with the men, he fell into step behind them. Father was in the lead, and Uncle Solomon, using the long pole he carried as a walking stick, walked beside Grandfather. The pole would be used to tie the lamb's dead carcass to when they brought it home.

The city streets were teeming with people who were pushing and shoving their way to the marketplace. At the far end of the market, men swarmed around wooden stalls bursting with the plump little lambs.

Some men struggled to climb over the wooden railings to make a selection. Others inside the pens waited anxiously to exit the gated area with their prized pick. The lambs, bleating loudly, added to the chaos.

"Son, your uncle and I are going to buy some rope,"

Father said. "Stay with your grandfather. He will go with you to make the selection. This year you have the honor of deciding which one will become our Seder meal."

Benjamin didn't want to do the choosing, but still he followed his grandfather to the stall. The smell of dung was strong.

"It's your choice," Grandfather said. "Pick a good one."

Benjamin stared at the animals. "Do I have to do this, Grandfather?"

"It's a tradition. Men select the meat for the meal."

Benjamin gritted his teeth and climbed over the rail into the pen. He bent down, wedged between two fat lambs. His throat tightened as their cries surrounded him. "Grandfather, I don't know what to do."

Grandfather crossed his arms and without a word, he entered the pen through the gate and made his way to Benjamin. "Stoop down and run your hands over them. Dig your fingers in and you'll be able to tell which one is small and tender," he said softly.

Benjamin sank his fingers into the thick wool of several bleating lambs. His stomach knotted, but he kept moving through the stall. Finally, he found an animal that seemed right. "This one's not too fat," he said.

Grandfather nodded his approval and left through the gate.

Father and Uncle Solomon appeared with a long section of rope.

Benjamin lifted the squirming lamb and made his way out of the pen. His captive prize bleated loudly, but he held the little fellow with a firm grip.

"Will this one do, Father?"

"It is up to you. Are you satisfied?"

Benjamin nodded.

Father handed him the rope. "Tie the cord around its neck. I will go pay the merchant."

"Make a noose and slip it over its head," Uncle Solomon said, leaning on the pole.

Putting the lamb down, Benjamin quickly made the loop and slid it over the head of the animal, who cried louder and louder. "Shhh," he said, stroking its head. Perhaps the little one knew its fate.

When Father returned, he said, "At the temple, we will enter the north courtyard through the side gate and give the lamb to the priest. They will do what has to be done."

They pressed their way through the streets, which were now packed with men who were taking their approved goods to the slaughter. Benjamin tugged gently at the rope, and the fidgety animal trailed behind him.

At the outer courtyard of the temple, the frantic cries all around him made Benjamin want to flee and take the innocent little one with him. But since this ritual was part of their tradition, he lead the lamb into the north courtyard.

Inside, Benjamin handed the animal over to the Chief Priest. The priest seized the rope and grabbed a knife from the bench beside him. Another priest came to assist. They flipped the lamb on its side. The Chief Priest shoved his knee against its stomach, and with one swift motion, he cut its throat. The two priests held the limp body over a metal pan, allowing the blood to drain completely.

A vivid image of his mother with blood seeping through her fingers flashed through Benjamin's mind. He felt lightheaded, but he took a deep breath. Then he glanced over to where Father, Grandfather, and Uncle Solomon were standing, talking. They acted as if nothing unusual was taking place.

Benjamin realized as a Jew, his mother would want him to carry on this tradition and he didn't want to fail to honor her memory.

At the end of the ritual, the Chief Priest set aside the blood to be used on the temple altar. He skinned the small animal and removed the innards. He handed Grandfather the fleece and tossed the innards on a growing pile. Then he sliced off a generous portion of meat for himself and handed Father the remaining carcass.

"Benjamin, grab hold of the lamb's legs. We need to tie them to the pole," Father said.

Benjamin nodded and did as he was told. Uncle Solomon took the pole he carried, and using the rope, he assisted Benjamin and Father in tying the legs to it.

As they left the courtyard, the lifeless body swayed back and forth on the pole between father and son. The hot sun beat down on the fresh meat. Benjamin stumbled on a rock and lost his balance. The carcass shifted.

Father shook his head. "Watch where you are stepping. If the meat drops in the dirt, you can be sure that Aunt Esther will not be pleased with us."

The thatched roof of their house appeared, and relief swept over Benjamin.

Aunt Esther met them at the front door. "I see you purchased a small one. It looks tender. We'll have a fine feast."

The carcass was carried inside and placed on the cutting block. Grandfather and Uncle Solomon washed their hands in a pan that Aunt Esther had set out.

Benjamin and Father did the same. No matter how hard he scrubbed, Benjamin's hands still had traces of blood.

"I invited our neighbors for the Seder meal," Father announced. "Rabbi Aaron's wife, Ruth, has been called away to care for her sick father. He and the children are alone."

"Rachel's coming for the Seder meal?" Benjamin asked as a smile crossed his face.

"It seems so. You can help me sweep the corners of the room," Aunt Esther said. "I don't want any crumbs of leavened bread left anywhere." She handed him a small pan. "Start by taking the yeast outside. It needs to be burnt. We don't want any reminder of the days of slavery. After you finish, you can scrub the cupboards."

"Auntie, slow down, there is plenty of time. I know what to do." His throat tightened as he thought about how many times he had helped his mother prepare the house for Passover.

"Dear boy, I'm sorry. I only want to make this Seder special just like your mother would have," she said tearfully.

"I'm sorry too, Auntie. I didn't mean to upset you. I know you'll make everything perfect for us." He leaned over and quickly kissed her cheek.

Wiping her eyes with the corner of her apron and smiling, she gave him a nudge. "Let's get busy, there's cleaning, cutting, and baking to do."

For the rest of the day, Benjamin rushed around while Aunt Esther gave him orders. Finally, the smell of cooked apples mixed with cinnamon became too strong to resist. Benjamin scooped up a big gob of the crushed fruit and shoved it in his mouth. Aunt Esther shook her finger. "Out of my kitchen!" She shoved him playfully.

By sundown, the feast was ready.

A knock on the door announced that the guests had arrived. Benjamin, dressed in a clean tunic, his hair neatly combed, opened the door. Rachel, standing with Daniel behind Rabbi Aaron, wore a brightly embroidered white festival dress. Her dark hair, shining in the late afternoon sun, was pulled back off her face.

"Do not keep our friends waiting at the door. Invite them to the table," Father said.

Benjamin wanted to say something clever to impress Rachel. Instead he stammered, "I'm glad – umm, glad you're here – umm, here to share in our Passover meal."

Rachel smiled. Her eyes sparkled. "It was kind of your father to ask us."

The table was elaborately set. They stood around it while Father introduced Uncle Solomon and Aunt Esther to Rabbi Aaron and the children. Rachel was across the table from Benjamin. Daniel fidgeted next to his father, tugging at the top of his tunic as usual. "Are we going to eat soon?" he whispered. His father nudged him with an elbow.

Aunt Esther lit the candles. Father cleared his throat, raised a cup of wine, and sang the blessing. At the end of the song, they sat down and Father handed an empty cup to Rabbi Aaron. "This is in honor of the prophet Elijah," he said.

The rabbi poured some of his wine into it and continued to pass it around the table. Everyone added some wine, symbolizing unity.

Small individual bowls of water were on the table for washing hands. Next, a lush green leaf was dipped into salt water. "This signifies the tears shed by the Israelites in bondage," Father said.

Aunt Esther broke a circle of flatbread into two pieces and wrapped the larger part in a cloth. Sometime during the meal, she, as an adult, would hide that half. Later the youngsters would be asked to find it. As a child, Benjamin loved doing this, but he didn't look forward to the childish ritual with Rachel here.

Father asked Rabbi Aaron to tell the Exodus story. While the rabbi spoke eloquently, Benjamin pictured the ancient past: God called Moses to set the Israelites free from Egyptian slavery; Moses and his brother, Aaron, went to the Pharaoh to have him release the Israelites from captivity; the Pharaoh refused; God sent down ten plagues on the Egyptians; Moses led God's people to the Red Sea where he divided the waters and directed the people across to safe land and freedom.

At the end of the story, Rachel, being the youngest, asked, "Why is tonight unlike all the other nights?"

Grandfather answered, "Because it is a sacred night where we recall God's love for His chosen people."

Aunt Esther rose and brought over a pitcher of water and again filled the small bowls. They washed their hands a second time. Benjamin saw her hide the piece of flatbread before she sat down.

Next, bitter herbs were dipped into a mixture of sweet apples and nuts. "This is in memory of the days of slavery in Egypt," Father said. "It represents the bricks and mortar the Jews were forced to make to build the Egyptians' homes." Following that, roasted eggs were passed around in recognition of new life.

Finally, it was time for the hidden flatbread to be found. Benjamin, Rachel, and Daniel got up from the table and wandered around the room, looking under the chairs, behind the oven, and in the shelves. Benjamin hung back and waited for one of the twins to find the bread.

A few minutes later Daniel shouted, "Here it is!" He grabbed the cloth from under a shelf and the bread flew out and slid across the floor. "Sorry," he said. Sweat trickled down his chubby face as he picked up the piece and wiped it off. Sticking it back in the cloth, he handed it to Aunt Esther and slipped back onto his seat at the table. Aunt Esther grinned and shook her head as she set it aside.

Benjamin and Rachel returned to their seats, exchanging a quick smile before they sat down.

Aunt Esther passed the lamb. Instead of a generous portion, Benjamin took a small piece, and pushed it to the side of his plate. He usually enjoyed the roasted flavor, but this year he thought it would catch in his throat if he tried to eat it. He could still hear the nervous bleating of the little creature.

The meal ended, and they continued the celebration by singing ritual songs. Grandfather played his wooden flute. Benjamin sang quietly, so he could hear Rachel's sweet, delicate voice among the others.

Finally, Grandfather laid the flute on the table and yawned. "That's enough for me. I'm full and tired."

The evening's festivity came to an end. Everyone thanked Aunt Esther for preparing the Seder meal. She hugged Daniel and Rachel, telling them to come again.

As soon as the men said their goodbyes, both father and son escorted the guests to the door. The minute they opened it, they heard loud shouts echoing through the night. From across the valley, flaming torches could be seen burning brightly.

"It sounds like there is trouble," Father said.

"I hate to tell you," Rabbi Aaron said, "but it has been whispered that the men of the Sanhedrin Council were sending out temple guards tonight to arrest Jesus.

The Council decided that they would take Jesus before the court and charge him with blasphemy. He went too far, claiming to be the Son of God."

Benjamin couldn't believe what he was hearing. "Father, how could they do this to such a holy man? Can't we do something to stop them?"

His father shook his head. "It is useless."

"As your father and I know, it is impossible to interfere with what the Sanhedrin has decided," Rabbi Aaron said. "It saddens me to think of what they are planning to do, but once they have made a decision nothing will stand in their way. Come, children, it is time to leave. There is nothing more we can do tonight."

"But..." Benjamin's protest dissolved under his father's warning glare.

Just before Rachel walked out the door, she whispered, "Shalom, Benjamin."

He smiled at her, but his thoughts were elsewhere. He had a plan, too. A plan that would have to wait until the household was asleep.

ELEVEN

THE DOGWOOD TREE

Benjamin planned to sneak into the city after everyone was asleep. He had to find out where the soldiers took Jesus. His heart raced when he thought about going alone, but fear wasn't going to stop him. He crawled into bed without undressing.

Although he fought to stay awake, his eyes kept closing and he soon fell into a deep sleep. In a dream, a pure white cloud drifted into his room and hovered above his bed.

The cloud glowed from the inside. Its light grew in intensity. Fascinated by the brightness, Benjamin reached up to touch it. To his amazement, a delicate figure stepped out. It was his mother. She wore a long white gown that swayed gracefully.

"God sent me to talk with you." She smiled and glided toward him.

Benjamin trembled with excitement. "I thought I'd never see you again!"

She pulled him into her arms. Benjamin breathed in her sweet fragrance.

"Son, God cares what happens to you," she said softly. "He feels your pain and knows your anger. Anger can turn to bitterness and can destroy your kind-hearted spirit. Forgive and you will be forgiven. Let go of the shame you feel about my death. It was not your fault. Always remember, you are loved. It matters that you are to love and to be love. And you are to love and serve God." She kissed him, and although he could still feel her arms around him, her image began to fade.

"Mother, don't leave me," he cried, grabbing to hold onto her. But she was gone, taking the light with her. He immediately felt himself falling through darkness. Then, hitting something hard, he awoke with a jolt. He was on the floor of his bedroom tangled in his blanket.

"Benjamin, what are you doing? You woke me," Father said, his voice heavy with sleep.

"Sorry, Father. I'm all right."

"Well, go to sleep. It will be morning soon."

Struggling to untangle himself, Benjamin realized the vision of his mother had been a dream. The words of forgiveness and love that she had spoken whirled in his mind.

Did he really have to let go of his shame? What about the soldier who killed his mother, did he have to forgive him too? And God? Did God really care and want his love?

His thoughts were spinning when one of Grandfather's loud snores broke into his confusion. He lay still for a moment, listening. Father's breathing was steady and even. Benjamin knew if he was going to leave for the city, it had better be now.

He crept out of the house. Stars speckled the night sky. He hurried through the olive grove and ran up the road, watching for loose stones.

The cold air chilled him and made his breathing raspy.

Once inside the city wall, he gulped hard to catch his breath. The streets were empty as he made his way to the marketplace. It was deserted too, but the sound of voices came from the street that led to the Antonia Fortress. He headed toward the noise.

In front of the fortress' large gate, people huddled around scattered fires. Benjamin joined them. He rubbed his hands together to get them warm. A man, using a crutch, hobbled over next to him. "Are they still holding Jesus inside?" he asked loudly.

"I don't know." Benjamin shrugged. "I just got here."

Leaning heavily on his crutch, the man said, "If they haven't released him by now, they never will. Some in the council see him as a threat to their laws."

Someone dropped a piece of wood onto the fire. Sparks shot up. In the explosion of light, Benjamin saw one of Jesus' friends nearby, but he couldn't remember his name.

The crippled man pointed a stubby finger. "You're Peter, aren't you? You're one of those who followed Jesus."

Peter backed away from the fire. "You're wrong. I don't know him,"

Benjamin couldn't believe what he heard. Why would Peter lie?

An old woman wrapped in a tattered shawl shook her gnarled fist. "I saw you with him."

"You're mistaken. I don't know the man." Peter took another step backward. He stopped within inches of Benjamin.

A broad-shouldered man grabbed the front of Peter's cloak. "You can't deny knowing him. You were with him while he preached in the marketplace."

"I tell you, I was never with him." Peter shoved the man's hand away. Turning, he collided with Benjamin. Their eyes met for a moment. Just then, a cock crowed in the distance. Peter glanced wild-eyed from side to side, and turning, he fled into the night.

The wooden gate of the fortress swung wide and a troop of soldiers marched out. They had spears in one hand and lit torches in the other.

The captain shouted, "There's nothing for you here. Go home." The soldiers advanced and drove the crowd away. People hurried off in every direction.

Benjamin raced down a side street, never looking back. He passed through the North Gate and hurried along the dark path. Why had Peter denied knowing Jesus? It didn't make any sense. Benjamin felt the sadness of that betrayal, and he ran faster, wanting to shake it off.

As he reached the olive grove, the sun peeked above the horizon. He rushed toward the house so he could crawl into bed before his father woke and discovered him missing.

Suddenly, a loud crack resonated through the air. It halted Benjamin in his tracks. In the haze of the morning light, he saw two palace guards near the dogwood tree. One swung an axe that gouged deep cuts into the tree's trunk; his muscles bulged, and woodchips went flying everywhere. The ear shattering noise erupted into the air.

"Stop!" Benjamin yelled. "What are you doing?"

The other guard blocked Benjamin with his spear. "Boy, you'd better leave. We've got orders to do this."

"That tree belongs to my grandfather. You can't cut it down!" Benjamin said.

"Look who's telling us what we can't do?" The guard laughed.

Determined to stop the destruction of Grandfather's beloved tree, Benjamin tried to push past him. But the guard grabbed the back of his tunic and swung him around. "We have a real fighter here," he said, shaking Benjamin like a sack of grain.

"Take your hands off my son," Father said, as he came running across the grove. Grandfather was following closely behind. The crashing blows from the axe must have carried all the way to the house.

The guard shoved Benjamin to the ground. "Take your boy, but keep him away from us. We have work to do."

Benjamin leaped to his feet. "You have no right to cut down our tree."

"Rights?" The guard grunted. "You Jews are the ones without rights."

"Get off my land, now," Grandfather demanded.

The guard laughed again, "All lands belong to Rome."

Grandfather grabbed the arm of the guard who was swinging the axe, but the guard turned and hit Grandfather on the side of the head with the blunt end of the axe's handle. Grandfather fell to his knees. A trickle of blood appeared above his eye.

Father rushed to Grandfather. He pulled a cloth from his sleeve, wiped the blood from the cut, and then tied the cloth around his forehead to stop the bleeding.

"Why are they doing this?" Grandfather asked. Tears brimmed in his eyes.

Father helped him to his feet. "We will never understand them. Let us go to the house and take care of your cut. There is nothing more we can do here."

"Not yet," Grandfather insisted, standing firm. "I won't go until they leave. This is my land, no matter what they say."

Benjamin slipped his arm through his grandfather's. Then the three of them watched helplessly while the guard's axe dug deeply into the tree trunk. Splinters of wood flew in every direction until, with a sharp crack, the dogwood crashed to the ground and a cloud of dust billowed up.

"You'll regret this," Benjamin said boldly.

"Regrets? We have no regrets. We're just following orders." The guards began to strip away the branches from the trunk.

They cut the tree into two large beams. Finally, the guards hefted the beams onto to their shoulders and dragged them up the road.

Grandfather sighed. "It's over."

"Let us go then," Father said. "We will clean up their mess later."

They walked arm-in-arm toward the house.

"Grandfather, I hate the Romans!"

Father frowned. "Hate is a strong word. I have lived under Roman Rule all my life. Violence is not the solution."

"They use violence. Why can't we?"

"If we do, we become like them. Do you want that?"

"Do we always have to do what's right?"

"That is what our faith teaches us."

When they reached the house, Uncle Solomon and Aunt Esther rushed out to meet them. "We were sleeping when we heard a loud crash. What happened to Grandfather's head?" Uncle Solomon asked.

"Soldiers chopped down the dogwood tree. Grandfather tried to stop them and a guard hit him with the handle of his axe."

Aunt Esther lifted the bloody cloth from the old man's head. "Come inside and let me care for that nasty cut."

Grandfather sat at the table while Aunt Esther cleaned his wound.

"I'm sorry we couldn't save your dogwood tree," Benjamin said, placing his hand on Grandfather's shoulder.

The old man patted Benjamin's hand. "We did all we could."

"I think you should rest," Uncle Solomon said. He and Aunt Esther helped Grandfather into the bedroom.

"Father, I went into the city last night while you were sleeping," Benjamin said, blurting the words out, and then quickly cupping his hand over his mouth.

His father's brows furrowed. "Why would you go alone? It is dangerous."

Benjamin slowly removed his hand. "I wanted to find out what they did with Jesus. He hasn't committed any crime. He isn't a criminal. I wanted to see if they would release him, but before I could find out anything, Roman soldiers drove us away from the fortress where he is being held."

"Son, even though I have not wanted you to get involved, it took courage to go into the city alone. I have always followed the Roman Rules because I feared for the safety of our family. I have allowed them to treat us badly. But today after I saw how the guards abused you and your grandfather, it is time I make a stand for our family."

"Father, are you saying that you are ready to fight against their cruelty?"

"I do not believe in violence, but I am ready to do what is right. If you still want to go into the city to find out what they have done with Jesus, I will go with you. I will not stand idly by any longer. I am tired of having to bow down to them."

Benjamin shook his head in disbelief. "Father, I'm sure the Sanhedrin Council will realize they've made a terrible mistake arresting Jesus. If we hurry, we can get to the city in time to see them set Jesus free."

TWELVE

CRUCIFIXION

Curiosity seekers packed into the city. Benjamin and his father, along with the crowd, advanced down the street toward Antonio Fortress.

A man who was wedged in beside Benjamin said, "The news of the arrest traveled quickly. I heard the trial already took place. They're bringing Jesus back to the fortress to be judged by the governor."

"Do you think Pilate will let him go, Father?" Benjamin asked.

"I am not sure if the authorities will release him without some sort of punishment."

At the fortress, the large door was open. Inside, Pontius Pilate was seated on an elaborate marble throne at the top of a long stairway.

"Look Father, Daniel and Rachel are standing near the bottom of the stairs with Rabbi Aaron," Benjamin said, pointing. "May we join them?"

Father nodded, and they pressed through the crowd.

People grumbled angry words and tension surrounded them as they passed.

Reaching the twins, Benjamin squeezed in between them. Rachel's face was somber. "I'm glad you're here," she said.

Daniel fidgeted. "How long before they bring Jesus out? Do you think they will free him?"

Benjamin shook his head. "I don't know. We'll have to wait and see."

"The results of the trial will be announced soon," Rabbi Aaron said.

A soldier dragged a man tied with a rope around his neck into the outer courtyard. A roar went up from the crowd.

Benjamin's jaw tightened. It was Jesus.

A second man was hauled into the courtyard with chains on his wrists. Another roar went up.

"Who's that?" Daniel asked.

Benjamin studied him. "I don't know. He looks familiar."

"He's tugging at the shackles." Rachel's eyes widened. "His arms are bleeding."

"That's Barabbas," Rabbi Aaron said. "They arrested him for leading a band of rebels in the uprising last month. He's being tried for treason."

"I've seen him before," Benjamin said, staring at the man. "He's the rebel that hit me the day Mother..." He stopped, the words stuck in his throat.

A hush came over the crowd. Above them on the

platform, Pilate stood and raised his hands. "I find this man, Jesus, not guilty."

"Father, does that mean he'll be set free?" Benjamin asked.

"It is hard to tell what will be decided."

Pilate walked over to a basin and dipped his hands into the water. "I wash my hands of this man," he announced. "Now you decide. I will free Jesus or the criminal Barabbas."

A small group of religious leaders who were huddled at the bottom of the stairs began to chant. "Free Barabbas! Free Barabbas!" Many of the people chanted with them.

"Why would they set a madman free?" Benjamin asked, shaking his head. "This can't be true," he shouted. "We must set Jesus free. Free Jesus! Free Jesus!"

Daniel and Rachel joined in, but their shouts were drowned out by those who cheered, "Barabbas! Barabbas! Free Barabbas!"

"Free Jesus! Free Jesus!" Benjamin, Daniel, and Rachel continued to shout.

An old man shook his bony fist in Benjamin's face. "Be quiet, boy. Jesus deserves to die."

Benjamin pushed the man's fist away. "Why? He hasn't done anything wrong."

Barabbas pulled violently at the chains on his wrists. A guard unlocked the manacles and shoved him into the crowd. His eyes shifted frantically like a wild animal released from a trap. He quickly disappeared into the cheering mob.

Pilate stood on the platform and shouted, "What do you want me to do with this man Jesus?"

The religious leaders began to shout, "Crucify him! Crucify him!" Soon others picked up the call. "Crucify him! Crucify him!"

Benjamin watched in horror as soldiers removed the rope from Jesus' neck and with it they bound his hands. They dragged him to a wooden post where they tied his wrists. A soldier yanked Jesus' clothing down to his waist. Another grabbed a whip that lay at the foot of the post. He gripped the long handle in his right hand, and with a snap of his wrist, the leather straps cut into Jesus' flesh. Some of the people cheered and others turned away.

Benjamin cringed at the sight of Jesus' bloody back. Daniel appeared dazed. Rachel, her face pale and wet with tears, stared straight ahead as if in a trance.

"Don't look," Benjamin said.

Rachel hid her face in her father's cloak.

"We should leave," Father said, taking hold of Benjamin's arm.

Benjamin bit down on his lower lip. "We can't desert him, no matter what happens."

After the last stroke of the whip hit, a soldier untied Jesus. He collapsed. The soldier tossed a purple robe over Jesus' shoulders. "See, he wears the color of a royal king."

"He's the King of the Jews," an elderly man said mockingly and he bowed down.

The soldier jerked off the purple robe and yanked Jesus' garments back up over his torn flesh.

A sour taste filled Benjamin's mouth.

One of the palace guards pressed a crown of thorns onto Jesus' head.

The elderly man bowed down again. "Hail, King Jesus!"

"Stop it," Benjamin yelled.

A soldier crossed the courtyard dragging a large wooden cross. Benjamin saw the familiar scar. He knew the soldier was Marcus.

Marcus stopped in front of Jesus and dropped the cross. He yanked Jesus up, lifted the cross, and placed it on Jesus' shoulder. Benjamin recognized the heavy beams. He was grateful that Grandfather didn't have to see his beloved dogwood tree being used in such a brutal way.

Marcus placed the rope around Jesus' neck again. He led him from the courtyard, through the jeering crowd and up the street toward the hill, Golgotha.

"Clear the way! Clear the way!" The guards hollered, pushing people aside to open a path.

The crowd surged forward, and Benjamin was shoved to the far side of the road. He looked for his father but couldn't see him anywhere. Daniel, Rachel, and Rabbi Aaron had disappeared into the crowd too.

The sun was hot. Sweat trickled down Benjamin's

back as the procession swept him along. Jesus fell under the weight of the cross. Benjamin wanted to run and help him up, but the guards blocked his way.

Marcus pulled a muscular man from the crowd. “You seem strong enough. Help him carry it!”

“That’s Simon a Cyrenian,” a man leaning on wooden crutches said. “Better him than me. I’m of little use to anyone.”

Benjamin felt helpless too.

Simon lifted one side of the cross on his broad shoulders. He reached down and pulled Jesus up. Some of the women lining the street were weeping. Jesus stared at a modest woman wearing a blue headscarf. He mouthed the word, “Mother.” Benjamin, reminded of his own mother, felt a sting of sadness.

Even with Simon’s help, Jesus fell again. Simon, under the weight of the cross, picked him up. Together they made their way outside the city walls and climbed the hill to Golgotha, the Place of the Skull.

At the top, they dropped the cross. A soldier shoved Simon aside. He slipped away unnoticed by most.

The soldiers tore off Jesus’ cloak and placed him onto the cross. They stretched out his arms and legs over the rough wood. A soldier picked up a hammer and nailed spikes into Jesus’ wrists and feet. With every powerful blow, Benjamin’s body jerked.

After Jesus was nailed to the cross, the soldier tacked a plaque to the crossbeam above his head. Four soldiers lifted the cross and dropped it into a freshly dug hole. The words chiseled on the plaque read, "JESUS OF NAZARETH, THE KING OF THE JEWS."

Two criminals hung on crosses on either side of Jesus. One of them shouted, "If you are truly the Son of God, save us!"

The other one said, "We deserve to die for our crimes. This man is innocent." He then pled, "Remember me when you come into your Kingdom."

Jesus looked tenderly at the man. "Today you will be with me in Paradise."

The man wept.

Benjamin trembled. Was it possible that Jesus and the man would be with God this very day?

A man from the crowd shouted, "Jesus, what sort of God do you serve? He leaves you to die with common thieves!"

Benjamin found his voice. "Be quiet. Leave him alone. Hasn't he suffered enough?"

The man scowled. "He claims to be the Messiah. Can he not save himself?"

Overhead, dark clouds rolled in. The sky grew black as night. Women wailed. Benjamin was afraid, but he couldn't leave. If God created a miracle and freed Jesus from this terrible death, Benjamin wanted to be there.

The woman Jesus had called Mother knelt down at the foot of the cross. Tears streaked her lovely face. The young man next to her was crying. He placed his arm around her shoulders.

Jesus looked down. "John, take my mother as yours. Mother, take John as your son."

His mother smiled through her tears.

Nearby, soldiers rolled dice for Jesus' cloak. One of them stopped long enough to place a wine-soaked sponge on a reed. He shoved it to Jesus' lips, but Jesus refused to drink.

A loud clap of thunder sounded in the distance.

Jesus lifted his eyes skyward. "It is finished. Forgive them, Father, for they know not what they do."

Benjamin shuttered and gasped for air. How could Jesus forgive them? He knew he never could.

Jesus' body slumped forward. It was over.

Standing below the cross, a centurion cried out in anguish, "We have crucified the Son of God, the Messiah."

Benjamin's stomach heaved. Bile rose in his throat, and he leaned over to spit it out. His head pounded. Tears burned his eyes, and he wiped them with his sleeve.

He looked up and saw the soldier, Marcus, on his knees with his head bowed. Was Marcus sorry for what he had done? It was too late. Marcus had led Jesus to his death.

Lightning flashed, thunder crashed, and rain poured down in torrents. The earth quaked, rocks shifted. A fierce wind uprooted trees. Spectators screamed and fled from the hill.

Benjamin, caught in the middle of the flight, was

shoved down the muddy path. At the bottom, he saw the city's large wall before him. He followed the outside of the wall around to the North Gate and ran toward home.

He didn't stop until he heard his name being called over the howl of the wind. "Benjamin, Benjamin, wait for us!"

Father, Rabbi Aaron, and the twins were coming toward him on the rain soaked road.

"Did you make it to the hill? It must have been terrible," Daniel said in a shaky voice.

Benjamin nodded and fell into his father's waiting arms.

"Thank God, you are safe," Father said.

Benjamin leaned into his father's chest.

Father held him tightly. "If anything ever happened to you, I do not know what I would do. Losing your mother was devastating, but to lose you too…"

"Don't worry, Father. I'm all right."

"It is time we get home," Rabbi Aaron said, his arms around both his children.

Father linked arms with Benjamin.

They were all soaked to the skin as they walked along in silence. The deluge of rain finally stopped, but the wind tore through the trees and roared a long mournful cry. It sounded as if the whole world was grieving the loss of Jesus.

At the twins' house, they quickly exchanged their goodbyes.

Benjamin and Father continued down the road. When they reached the house, Uncle Solomon met them at the door. "Hurry inside. We've been so worried. The storm frightened us."

Aunt Esther hugged Benjamin. "Dear boy, are you all right?"

Benjamin nodded. "Auntie, where's Grandfather?"

"Still resting. He's been waiting for you to come home. He's anxious to hear about the outcome of the trial."

Grandfather sat up as everyone came into the bedroom. Benjamin knelt by the bed, dreading how he would explain the tragic news of Jesus' death. Finally he blurted out, "The beams from our dogwood tree – the Roman soldiers used them as a cross. They nailed Jesus to it. He hung there until he died."

Aunt Esther gasped, and Uncle Solomon took her in his arms and held her tightly.

Grandfather clutched Benjamin's hand. "That's enough. You don't have to go any farther."

"Grandfather," Benjamin said, his voice quivering, "why did the religious leaders want Jesus dead?"

"Perhaps it's because more and more people believed he was the Messiah. They couldn't have that."

Benjamin laid his head in his grandfather's lap. "If Jesus was the one God sent to save us, and now he's dead, then there's no hope for any of us."

THIRTEEN

RESURRECTION

Three days had passed since Jesus' death, but the sight of him hanging on the cross continued to haunt Benjamin's dreams. He woke in a sweat and rubbed his eyes to get rid of the stark image. Grandfather's raspy, sleep-ridden snores came from his cot, and Father's deep breathing could be heard across the dark room.

A loud knock at the front door startled Benjamin. Who would be visiting at such an early hour?

His father must have heard it too, because he got up, slipped on his robe, and went quickly into the outer room. Benjamin tossed back his covers, pulled on his tunic, and followed.

By now, father had lit an oil lamp. He held it in his hand as he stood at the door. Rabbi Aaron was standing outside in the dark. The twins were right behind him.

"Come in out of the cold," Father said, while ushering the three of them inside the house.

Grandfather came from the bedroom, yawning. "Who's here so early?" he asked.

"I am sorry to disturb your family before dawn," Rabbi Aaron said. "I have to go into the city this morning. My wife, Ruth, is returning from Ein Karem. Her father has recovered from his illness. Daniel will go with me, but I wonder if Rachel could stay with you?"

"Of course, she is always welcome," Father said, smiling at Rachel. But Rachel did not smile back. Her lips were pressed together tightly. Why did she look so unhappy?

Aunt Esther and Uncle Solomon came into the room. "Is everything all right?" Aunt Esther asked sleepily.

Rabbi Aaron nodded. "I told my wife, on her return, I would meet her at the temple. She is coming back today. I am afraid she is not aware of the events that have taken place during her absence."

"I don't understand why I can't go with you," Rachel said, scowling.

"I have already told you. I was in the city yesterday, and soldiers were patrolling near Jesus' tomb. Some were even standing guard there. It is no place for a girl."

Rachel stomped over and stood next to Aunt Esther, who smiled and placed an arm around the girl.

"Why are soldiers guarding the tomb?" Uncle Solomon asked, scratching his bald head.

"It is rumored that Jesus' followers are going to steal his body," Rabbi Aaron replied.

"What foolishness!" Grandfather said, while fingering the cut on the side of his head.

Daniel tugged Rabbi Aaron's sleeve. "Could Benjamin come with us?"

"Father, could I?" Benjamin pleaded. He desperately wanted to find out what was happening in the city.

"I do not know, Son. It could be dangerous. What do you think, Aaron?"

"I plan to take the back streets to avoid running into the soldiers. We will not go anywhere near Jesus' tomb. We should be safe enough."

Benjamin's father heaved a heavy sigh. "I am afraid there is no such thing as safe enough these days."

"You may be right, Samuel, but the soldiers are only looking for those who traveled with Jesus."

"Since I trust that you know your way around the city, Aaron, I will allow Benjamin to go along. I will pray that God watches over all of you and keeps you safe."

"Thank you, Father," Benjamin said, feeling a twinge of excitement.

"Be sure to listen to Rabbi Aaron. Do exactly what he says."

"I will. I promise."

"And I promise that we'll stay close to my father," Daniel said, putting a hand on Benjamin's shoulder.

Rabbi Aaron went to the door. "We will not be long."

As they left, Benjamin saw Rachel whispering to Aunt Esther. Aunt Esther frowned and shook her head.

Outside, the moon cast a bright light on their path. Rabbi Aaron led them through the olive grove and up the dirt road toward Jerusalem.

Benjamin was walking closely behind Daniel when he heard a rustling noise. He turned just in time to catch a glimpse of a slender figure that darted behind a clump of bushes.

He grabbed his friend's sleeve. "We're being followed," he whispered. "I think it's your sister Rachel."

The two of them stopped and peered into the shadows.

Daniel shook his head. "I knew she'd come after us."

"Should we stay here until she comes out of hiding?"

"I don't want to lose sight of my father. I'm sure he thinks we're right behind him. You can stay if you want to. I'll catch up with him. We'll wait for you by the wall outside the North Gate. Try to talk Rachel into going back. Maybe she'll listen to you. She never listens to me." Daniel shrugged, and then hurried after his father.

Benjamin slipped behind a pile of rocks. After a few moments, Rachel snuck out from the bushes. As she crossed in front of him, he reached out and gently touched her arm.

She let out a piercing screech.

"Rachel, it's me, Benjamin. I'm sorry I frightened you. I thought you were supposed to stay at the house?"

"She's my mother too!" Her voice was shaky.

"Don't cry," Benjamin said, reaching for her hand.

She pulled away. "I'm not crying. I'm angry. Everyone treats me like a child."

Benjamin nodded, he knew how that felt. "Don't be mad at me. It's your father who's going to be upset with you."

"He's too protective. I told Aunt Esther I had to go. She tried to talk me out of it, but I begged her. She finally realized it was no use arguing with me. Not wanting me to be on the road alone, she insisted I hurry to catch up with my father."

"Didn't my father try to stop you?"

"He was praying for your safety with your uncle and grandfather. They didn't see me leave."

"You should go back to the house. They'll all be worried."

"I can't go back. You can't make me." Rachel placed her hands on her hips. Benjamin smiled to himself. As a little girl, she did the same thing whenever she wanted to get her own way.

"Well, if your mind's made up, I guess no one can stop you. Come on, since you're not going back, we'd better not keep your father waiting." He grabbed her hand, and this time she didn't pull away. They started off at a slow run.

Outside the North Gate, Rabbi Aaron and Daniel were hidden in the shadow of a cedar tree. When Rachel and Benjamin approached, Rabbi Aaron heaved a heavy sigh. "I should have known better. You are stubborn, like your mother."

Rachel lowered her eyes. "I had to come."

"I know, I know. But we must hurry. We are late enough. Your mother may already be at the temple."

Overhead, silhouettes of a few soldiers showed against the early morning sky as they patrolled on the upper walkway of the limestone wall.

"Let's get out of here, Father, before we're seen," Daniel said, heading to the North Gate.

Inside the city walls, they made their way down deserted streets. "Stay close together," Rabbi Aaron whispered.

At the marketplace, blue hues of the morning's light splashed across the horizon. The market appeared empty with no sign of any soldiers.

Down near the temple's gate, a short, stout figure emerged and hurried toward them. "Mother!" Rachel cried.

"Shhh!" Rabbi Aaron's finger was on his lips.

His wife rushed to his side. "What's going on? There doesn't seem to be anyone in the city. Something's dreadfully wrong."

"Do not worry, Ruth," Rabbi Aaron said as he hugged her. "I will explain later."

At the far end of the square, Benjamin spotted a patrol of Roman soldiers. "Rabbi Aaron," he said, nodding in that direction. "What should we do?"

"I do not think they have seen us yet. Quickly, this way." Rabbi Aaron hurried them into a narrow passageway and down a side street. After that, every time they saw soldiers, the rabbi led them in a different direction. Before long, they had traveled away from the North Gate and were in the upper part of the city.

Benjamin's heart raced. What would happen to them if they were caught?

Shouts came from directly ahead of them. Rabbi Aaron hurried them all through a gate and into a small courtyard.

"The man who lives here is a friend," Rabbi Aaron said. "He lives upstairs. We will ask to stay with him until evening. When it gets dark, we can leave the city safely."

Benjamin knew his father would worry if they were late, but he didn't say anything. Rabbi Aaron wouldn't have stopped if he didn't think it was important.

They crossed the courtyard and entered a dark hallway. In front of them, a stairway led up to a closed door. Reaching the top, Rabbi Aaron knocked softly. Moments later, they heard the click of a lock, and the door opened a crack.

"Who's there?" a husky voice asked.

"It is Rabbi Aaron, I am looking for Ezra. We are friends."

"What do you want with him?"

"We need a safe place to stay. My wife just returned from Ein Karem where she was caring for her sick father. We met her at the temple and were returning home but soldiers are everywhere."

The door opened wider. To Benjamin's surprise, Peter was standing behind it. What was he doing here?

"You're a long way from the temple," Peter said. His eyes seemed troubled.

"In trying to stay clear of the soldiers, we traveled away from the North Gate where we first entered the city," Rabbi Aaron said. "We will make our way back home after it is dark."

Peter moved aside. "Come in. Ezra's inside with the others, praying."

They stepped into a small room that was dimly lit with a few scattered oil lamps. Peter closed and locked the door behind them.

Groups of men were seated on the floor praying. Benjamin recognized some who had been with Jesus in the marketplace.

In the corner of the room, women sat with their heads bowed. The woman Jesus had called Mother, that day at Golgotha, was there with her hands folded in her lap.

Ezra got up and came over. "Rabbi Aaron, I overheard your conversation with Peter. We are praying for the safety of our people. Will you join us?"

"We would be honored," Rabbi Aaron said. He introduced his wife and the children, and then waited with Peter while Ezra led Ruth and Rachel to where the women sat. Benjamin saw an open spot near the wall. He tugged Daniel's sleeve, and they both went over and sat down.

Once everyone was settled, Rabbi Aaron and Peter sat with Ezra and his group of men. Benjamin leaned his back against the wall.

Why were Jesus' companions here praying? And Peter? Only John and Jesus' mother were at Golgotha. All the others had deserted him. What brought them back together?

The men began to chant, "O Lord, I love you, you are my tower of strength, you are my stronghold, my redeemer, my..."

The sound of pounding on the door startled Benjamin and stopped the chanting. A woman's voice from outside called, "Let me in! Let me in!"

Peter jumped up and rushed to the door. He unlocked and opened it a crack. A woman with long, flowing black hair pushed her way in. Her face was flushed, and her cheeks were wet with tears. "He's alive! He's alive!"

"Mary, what are you saying?" Peter asked.

"Jesus, he's alive. I've spoken with him."

Benjamin stared at the frantic woman, as did everyone else.

A man sitting by Benjamin whispered, "Mary Magdalene's grief at the loss of Jesus has driven her mad."

"Calm down, Mary," Peter said, taking a gentle hold of her arm.

"I went to the tomb. It was open. The burial cloth lay folded on the slab inside."

"Mary, weren't soldiers there?" Peter asked.

"No, not that I saw." She was breathing rapidly. "There was only an angel who greeted me saying, 'He is no longer here. He has risen!' In the garden, I saw a man. I thought it was the gardener, but then he spoke and I knew it was Jesus. He said, 'Go and tell the others that I have risen.' I ran all the way here!"

Benjamin had seen Jesus hanging on the cross with his own eyes. This couldn't be true. Was the woman crazy?

Peter released Mary, and went to where Jesus' mother sat. He knelt beside her. "Could what Mary said be true?"

Her eyes met Peter's. "Why can't you believe? It's just as he foretold. He has come back to us."

Benjamin's thoughts were spinning. What was happening? How could Jesus be alive? Had God created a miracle after all?

"I don't understand." Peter seemed dazed.

"What's to understand?" Mary asked. "He's alive. That's all that matters."

"This isn't possible." Peter shook his head.

"Why?" Mary argued. "He brought Lazarus back after four days."

Jesus' mother nodded. "Mary tells the truth. But my son will not be with us for long."

"Why do you say that?" Peter pressed his fingers against his forehead.

"While praying, my son appeared to me in a vision.

He told me he would be with us for forty days. After that, he will return to his Father in Paradise."

Peter's shoulders sagged. "If he's not going to stay, why did he return?"

"He came back to show us that he has overcome death. Those who believe and follow the path he has set before them will do the same. They will be granted eternal life."

"Before they arrested him, I believed he was the Messiah. Why did I doubt?"

"Peter," Jesus' mother said, taking his hand, "trust what my son has told you. Go with Mary. See for yourself that the tomb is empty. Maybe then, you will be convinced of the truth."

"Will it be safe?" Peter asked.

"There is nothing to fear. With my son no longer there, the soldiers will have abandoned the tomb. Go now."

Peter and Mary left together. Ezra locked the door behind them. Benjamin wanted to go too. He wanted to know for certain that Jesus was alive. Why did Peter get to go? He didn't deserve to see the empty tomb after he lied about knowing Jesus and later deserted him when he was crucified.

A man sitting close to Benjamin leaned over to a man beside him, and said," Do you think Jesus' mother actually saw him in a vision?"

"She probably fell asleep and dreamed he spoke to her," the man answered.

Jesus' mother looked up. "It was not a dream. One day everyone will understand why God sent Jesus to earth. For now, let us continue praying. We have a lot to be thankful for. My son has come back from the dead." Her face looked serene. She lowered her head and resumed praying silently.

The men bowed their heads sheepishly and began chanting softly. Even Daniel joined in. Across the room, Rachel's lips were moving in silent prayer. Benjamin remained silent too, but his thoughts ran rampant.

If Jesus was really alive, would he gather an army to defeat the Romans? Was that why he had come back?

Whatever the reason for his return, Benjamin knew he wanted to be a part of it.

FOURTEEN

THE APPEARANCE

In the upper room, the men continued to chant. Benjamin squirmed, his back aching from leaning against the hard wall. What had happened to Peter and Mary? Were they ever coming back? Would he ever find out why the tomb was empty?

Across the room, Rachel's head was still lowered in prayer. Benjamin stared, she looked so lovely.

Daniel slid over and bumped Benjamin. "My throat's dry, and I'm starving! Do you think they'll feed us?"

Benjamin shook his head. "I don't know, but I do know that you're always hungry!"

Just then, some of the older women started to unpack food from their cloth bundles. A few of them passed among the men, giving out bread and cheese. The praying ceased as soon as everyone began to eat.

Daniel was handed a piece of bread and he downed it with a few bites. One of the women offered Benjamin some, but he refused. Food was the last thing on his mind.

Rachel, carrying a water bucket, stopped in front of Benjamin. Scooping a dipper-full, she handed it to him.

As he drank, Benjamin watched her over the rim. Their eyes met. She smiled and didn't look away. His hand shook and he almost dropped the ladle as he handed it back. "Thank you," he said, swallowing hard.

"Don't forget me?" Daniel said,

Rachel dipped the ladle again. "Be patient, you're next. And don't spill on yourself."

After everyone was served, there were quiet conversations in some of the groups, while others ate in silence.

When they had all finished eating, some of the men began refilling the oil lamps that were scattered around the room. The women packed the leftovers and returned to silent prayer. The men began to chant once more until they were interrupted by a knock at the door.

Ezra got up and unlocked it, and then he opened it a crack. "It's Peter and Mary. They've come back."

As soon as they were inside, he closed and locked the door again.

Peter quickly went and knelt by Jesus' mother.

"What did you see?" she asked.

"An empty tomb, just as Mary said. Only his burial cloth remained." He handed it to her. "Do you think Jesus will ever forgive me for doubting him?"

She embraced the cloth, and before she could answer Peter's question, an illuminated figure passed through the locked door and lit up the room. Jesus stood among them, light radiating from him. A pure white garment covered his body.

Benjamin rubbed his eyes. Was this real or was he imagining it?

Jesus placed a hand on Peter's shoulder. "My friend, I have already forgiven you."

Peter bowed his head. "You are truly the Messiah."

Jesus smiled. His face, soft and gentle, glowed. He bent down and kissed his mother's cheek. "Peace to you, Mother."

"And to you, my Son."

Benjamin listened intently. He couldn't take his eyes off of Jesus.

Jesus approached Mary. "You did as I asked. You are a faithful disciple."

"You've taught us well," she said. "You've been an example of how we should love one another."

Jesus walked around the room. "Do not be afraid. It has been written that the Messiah would die and rise on the third day. You are witnesses to this event. Go and preach it as good news to all you meet. Those who are willing to believe what they hear will have eternal life."

Everyone stared at him.

Benjamin felt the stir of a warm, gentle breeze. Was Jesus a ghost? Surely, he must be a ghost.

Jesus held out his wounded wrists toward Benjamin. "I am not a ghost. See for yourself."

Benjamin's hands trembled. He couldn't bring himself to touch the holes that went completely through Jesus' flesh.

"Believe what you see and what you hear from me," Jesus said. "But do not be fooled. Others may try to deceive you. Your eyes can be tricked and so can your ears. But when my Spirit dwells in you, truth will reside in your heart and you will never be misled."

Jesus walked to the center of the room. "I promised to send the Spirit of the living God, the Comforter who will remain with you always." He lifted his hands and prayed, "Be baptized with the Holy Spirit of truth that will teach and guide you in all my ways."

As soon as the words were spoken, Benjamin felt an intense heat course through his body. A feeling of love washed over him that he could hardly contain. His fear drained away and was replaced with a feeling of courage that he had never experienced before. Benjamin glanced around and to his amazement everyone's face appeared to glow. A powerful wave of joy swept over the room. Benjamin started to laugh, as did several others.

The laughter quickly subsided because the oil lamps flickered and died. Darkness descended onto the room. A few seconds later, the flames in the lamps flared back up. Jesus was no longer with them. Benjamin wondered if he would ever see him again.

Peter raised his voice, giving praises to God. The others joined in. Jesus had set Peter free from guilt. In his heart, Benjamin felt his anger toward Peter slipping away, and the shame about his mother's death was no longer so heavy on his heart.

Rachel appeared at Benjamin's side. Her eyes sparkled like gems dropped in a pool of clear water. "You look so happy," she said, smiling.

Without thinking, Benjamin jumped up and grabbed her into a hug. Stunned by his own action, he quickly released her.

"I'm—I'm sorry!" His knees went weak. Rachel blushed and hurried to where her mother stood embracing Rabbi Aaron.

Just then Daniel grabbed Benjamin into a bear hug. "I believe now. I truly believe."

"Me too," Benjamin said.

The whole room was filled with laughter.

After awhile the people began to pray and give thanks for Jesus' appearance.

Once the prayers ceased Rabbi Aaron came over to Benjamin and Daniel. "It is late. I believe it will be safe to leave now. Ruth, Rachel, it is time to start for home."

They gathered at the door with Peter and Ezra to say their goodbyes. Then Ezra unlocked the door.

"If you head south to the Dung Gate, you're least likely to run into any soldiers," Peter said. "That's the quickest way out of the city."

As they made their way down the stairs, Benjamin felt strange and yet wonderful. Outside night had settled in.

"Let us stay together," Rabbi Aaron said, taking his wife's arm. "If we see any soldiers, keep moving unless we are ordered to stop."

Rachel walked between Benjamin and Daniel. They moved quickly through the dark streets, passing decorative walls that surrounded the homes of the wealthy. Shutters on storefronts were closed tightly.

Finally, the Dung Gate came into sight. But before they could pass through the gate, a soldier, carrying a spear, stepped from the doorway of one of the storefronts.

"Halt!" he commanded. Benjamin saw the protruding jaw and recognized Thaddeus, Marcus' friend. "Where are you going at this late hour?" Thaddeus asked.

Rabbi Aaron placed his arm around his wife's shoulder. "We are going home."

"I really care more about where you've been. That's what interests me." Thaddeus pointed the tip of his spear at Rabbi Aaron. "Have you been to the tomb?"

"What tomb?"

"Don't pretend you don't know what I'm talking about."

Feeling fearless, Benjamin stepped between Rabbi Aaron and Thaddeus. "Why would we risk going to the tomb?" he asked. "We heard it's off limits."

Thaddeus tapped Benjamin's chest with his spear. "If you weren't there, where were you?"

"Not at the tomb," Benjamin replied.

"Well, somebody was there. Jesus' body has been stolen! And I'm going to find out who did it."

"Thaddeus! Let them pass!" A man cloaked in a brown hooded robe stepped out of the shadows. "Can't you see it's just a rabbi with his family? How would they know anything?"

The hood shifted, revealing Marcus' scarred face. What was he doing here? Why was he coming to their defense? And why was he out of uniform?

Thaddeus lowered his spear. "Marcus, don't you know an order has been given to bring you in for desertion?"

"I know, but as my friend will you hide me until I can get safely out of the city. Will you help me escape?"

"I can't. I've been assigned to find whoever stole Jesus' body."

"Do these Jews look like they could steal a body? Let them go and help me. You're the only person I can trust."

"If it was anyone else but you, Marcus, I wouldn't. But for you – well, you saved my life in battle many times."

Thaddeus swung his spear toward Rabbi Aaron. "If I find you sneaking around again, you can be sure I'll arrest all of you. Come Marcus, I know a safe place for you." He put an arm around Marcus' shoulders and the two disappeared down a dark alleyway.

They all breathed a sigh of relief.

"We've been blessed by God," Ruth said. "Who knows what that soldier would have done if that hooded man hadn't come along."

Benjamin wondered about Marcus' sudden change. Was he a blessing now instead of a curse? This was hard to believe.

"Let us hurry along before we are stopped by another soldier," Rabbi Aaron said as he led the small group through the Dung Gate.

They took the dark path that led around the city wall to the North Gate. From there, they made their way down the dirt road.

As they approached the twin's house. Benjamin said, "I'm going to take a shortcut through the olive grove. I'm certain by now that my father is worried. I was supposed to be home hours ago."

"Do you want me to go with you?" Rabbi Aaron asked.

"No, I'll be all right."

Benjamin took off running. As he came near the long stone wall that separated the grove from the house, he saw a man wearing a white robe standing in the shadows by one of the olive trees.

At first Benjamin thought of jumping over the wall to get away from the stranger, but he realized he wasn't afraid. "What do you want?" he asked.

The man stepped into the moonlight. His face looked serene. "May I talk to you about the events that occurred today?"

"What do you mean?" Benjamin took a step back.

"I mean, what you experienced at Ezra's house."

"How do you know where I was? And if you were there, I would have remembered you. I don't know you. Are you trying to trick me?"

"I would never do that, Benjamin."

"How do you know my name?"

"I know all about you. I am here to talk to you about the Holy Spirit, whom you experienced for the first time in the upper room today. With this new knowledge of the Holy Spirit, you will tell others about what you have seen and heard this day."

Benjamin shook his head. "Will anyone believe me?"

"That is the risk you take by becoming a disciple."

"A disciple? Who are you?"

The man held out his hands and exposed his wounded wrists.

Benjamin's eyes opened wide. "Jesus! Is it really you?"

"Yes."

"Why didn't I recognize you?"

"You were not meant to. You saw only what I wanted you to see. Although you did not recognize me, you were not afraid. You are learning that you do not have to fear anything, now that my Holy Spirit is with you and protecting you. Remember, you have not chosen God, God has chosen you."

"God chose me?" Benjamin's mind raced. "Why would God choose me? I haven't prayed to Him since the death of my mother."

"One day you will understand that God has always had a plan for your life. Once you have learned that, you will help others to discover God's design for their own lives."

"I don't think I will be able to do what you ask. I don't know what to do."

"That is right. That is why I will send the Holy Spirit to visit you and take you on a journey."

"I can't go on a journey. I'm expected at home. I'm already late."

Jesus laughed. "It is not that kind of journey. You will see. Have faith. All things are possible with God."

"Son, is that you?"

Benjamin turned and saw his father in the doorway of their home with a lit oil lamp in his hand.

"Yes, Father, I'm here."

When he turned back to invite Jesus into the house, he was gone. A shaft of moonlight shone on the spot where he had stood moments ago.

Benjamin felt confused. He hadn't grasped much of what Jesus had told him, but he was eager to learn about becoming a disciple.

He jumped the stone wall and ran to the house, all the while wondering when the Holy Spirit would come to take him on the journey.

FIFTEEN

THE PROMISE

The cool night air sent a chill through Benjamin as he ran to the house. His father was waiting in the doorway. "Son, we were worried that something dreadful had happened to you. Rabbi Aaron told me you would not be long. Was his wife late? Is that what kept you?"

"She was at the temple when we got there, but soldiers were everywhere. We had to find a place to hide until nightfall."

His father put his hand on Benjamin's shoulder. "It is cold out here. Let us get inside, and then you can tell us everything."

As they entered, Grandfather and Uncle Solomon, who were seated at the table on floor cushions, stood up. Aunt Esther, at the oven stirring a pot of what smelled like barley soup, dropped the spoon and hurried to Benjamin.

She placed her hands on both sides of his face and

gazed into his eyes. "There's something different about you. I can tell."

"Auntie, I saw Jesus. He's alive."

"What are you saying?" She touched his forehead. "You're hot. Are you delirious?"

"No, Auntie."

"Jesus is alive?" Uncle Solomon rubbed his bald head. "How can that be?"

"The boy wouldn't lie," Grandfather said, shaking his head.

Father led Benjamin to the table. "Sit down so you can tell us what happened."

Everyone took a seat and waited for Benjamin to speak. He was quiet for a few minutes because he didn't know where to start. But as he began to talk, the words spilled out so fast, he could hardly keep up with them. He told them what had taken place in the upper room and about the run-in with the two soldiers before they left the city.

When he finished, no one said a word. Did they believe him? He had lived it, and it didn't seem real. If they didn't believe these events, how could he explain his meeting with Jesus in the olive grove? He decided to keep that encounter to himself until he could come to some understanding of what Jesus had told him.

Father got up from the table and paced. "This does not seem possible. Still, if you say Jesus is alive, and you saw him, it must be true."

Grandfather stroked his beard. "Of course he's telling the truth. Benjamin wouldn't make this up."

"You believe me?"

They all nodded. Benjamin breathed a deep sigh of relief.

"With the return of Jesus, the people will have to accept that he's the Messiah," Uncle Solomon said.

"I wouldn't be so certain," Grandfather replied. "Some people have to see for themselves before they accept the truth."

"Benjamin, dear boy, can I fix you something? The barley soup is hot. I'll get some for you."

"No, Auntie. I'm just tired."

"Then to bed with you."

"We can continue this discussion in the morning," Father said.

Benjamin stood and slowly went into his bedroom. The darkness of the room encompassed him. Too tired to remove his tunic, he lay down on his cot and pulled a blanket over his head. He tried to sleep, but the days' events kept racing through his mind.

"Benjamin."

"Is that you, Father?" he asked, peeking out from under the cover.

Nobody answered. Benjamin got up and stumbled to the bedroom door.

The adults were still talking in the outer room. "Father, did you call?"

"No, why do you ask?"

"I heard my name. I thought it was you."

"Go to sleep," Aunt Esther said. "You're overtired."

He went back and tumbled into bed.

"Benjamin." There it was again.

"Who is it?" he demanded, glaring into the dark.

Aunt Esther came in the room carrying an oil lamp. "What's troubling you, Benjamin?"

"I keep hearing my name being called."

Aunt Esther held up the lamp and glanced around. "There's no one here. Are you certain you heard your name?"

"Yes, Auntie, I'm sure."

Aunt Esther raised her eyebrows and nodded. "Benjamin do you remember the account in the Torah where God called Samuel by name? I wonder..."

"Auntie, Jesus did say he would send the Holy Spirit to visit me. Do you think it could be…?"

"If it's the Holy Spirit, and you're being called like Samuel, you'd better listen." Aunt Esther leaned down and spoke softly, "Try to sleep. If you're being called to serve God, you'll know soon enough."

Aunt Esther kissed his forehead and left. The room was dark again. Benjamin yanked the blanket over his head. It was quiet for a while. Then he heard his name a third time.

"Benjamin."

"Who are you?"

"I am the voice of the Holy Spirit, the one promised."

Benjamin sat up and squinted into the darkness. Was this another dream?

"You are not dreaming, Benjamin. I am as real as your next thought and your next breath. With the death of your mother, you felt the pain of loss. You also experienced the anguish of seeing Jesus suffer and die. In the upper room, during Jesus' appearance, he gave the Holy Spirit to all those present. You received me too, that is why I am here. There is nothing to fear."

"I'm not afraid. Jesus said he would send you to take me on a journey."

"Yes, Benjamin, it is a journey, from birth to the present. During this journey your whole life will flash before your eyes."

Questions filled Benjamin's head, but he wanted to concentrate on every word from the Holy Spirit. He wanted to learn and to understand.

The voice was silent for a moment, and then it said, "Benjamin, are you ready?"

Benjamin nodded, and at that instant, his dark room flooded with light. Images appeared and passed before his eyes. He saw himself as a newborn cradled in his mother's arms. His father was standing nearby. "We will call him Benjamin. The name means the right hand of God. He will grow strong in faith and serve God."

His mother kissed his cheek and whispered, "I love you, little one." He smiled, remembering how wonderful it was to be called "little one" by his mother.

His life continued to unfold: from infancy, where he felt the warmth of his mother's arms; to childhood, where he was taught lessons from his father. He could still hear his father's voice, saying, "Learn our laws well, son. When you become a man, you will teach them to others."

Scenes emerged from his childhood that included his friends, Daniel and Rachel. He couldn't stop grinning at how little and full of mischief they all were.

Next, there were sights from when he and his parents moved in with his grandfather after the death of his grandmother. They showed Grandfather teaching him how to prune and care for the olive trees. Many evenings they would sit, just the two of them, beneath the dogwood tree, and Grandfather would tell him family stories.

As each event of Benjamin's life played out before his eyes, he relaxed and enjoyed them. But when his mother's death appeared, instead of standing by silently and choking back his tears, Benjamin cried until the pain of her loss was washed away.

The vision of the time he met Jesus in the temple was vivid as he once again felt the heat from the touch of His cloak. While seeing each of their encounters reappear, emotions were evoked that made Benjamin both happy and sad.

Finally the occurrence when Jesus talked to him in the olive grove sprang up before him. When that image faded, the voice of the Holy Spirit called his name, one more time. The room that had been filled with light plunged into darkness again.

"Your old life has passed away," the voice said. "It is time to begin anew. Now, Jesus would like you to visit his tomb."

"But Jesus' tomb is empty. His body is gone."

"You can choose to go or not. You always have a choice. Are you willing to see for yourself?"

Benjamin released an intense sigh and nodded.

To his astonishment, he immediately found himself outside the tomb. The large stone, once rolled away from the opening, now covered the entrance. Before he could take another breath, he passed right through the rock. Once inside, an aura of light flooded the tomb. It came from Jesus who was seated on a long stone slab. "Come sit with me," He said, patting the place next to Him.

Awed by Jesus' presence, Benjamin sat down willingly. His mother's tomb had been dark and damp with a musty smell. In here, Jesus' light reflected off the walls, and the air smelled fresh, like a field of wildflowers.

"Why isn't your tomb dark, and why did you want to meet me here?" Benjamin asked.

"I wanted to show you that no matter where you find me, there is light. Where I am, there is no darkness. You may find yourself in dark places, but I will always bring light to them."

"I asked the Holy Spirit about being a disciple. He

said I would find out soon enough. Will I become one now?"

Jesus laughed warmly. "Have patience, Benjamin. Discipleship takes time. First, let me explain to you the most difficult part of being a disciple."

"What is that?"

"It is the ability to forgive. This means that you have to find it in your heart to let go of all the hurt, pain, and injustices others have caused you."

An image of his mother being stabbed flashed across his mind. "I don't think I can do that."

"Benjamin, once you forgive those who have hurt you, you are released from the pain they have inflicted on you. It also frees the person who hurt you. You have been set free from your past. Free others. Forgiveness with love is the way to live. Do you understand?"

"I don't know." Benjamin rubbed his eyes. "I'm not sure I can ever forgive certain people."

"It will not be easy, but at least you are honest about how you feel. You look tired. It is time for you to sleep. Remember to call upon the Holy Spirit whenever you need guidance. He is always with you."

Tiredness washed over Benjamin, and he closed his eyes. The next thing he knew it was morning, and he awoke in his bedroom, alone and completely rested. Like all the other mornings since Aunt Esther's arrival, he smelled bread baking. His surroundings seemed the same, but he knew he was different.

He jumped out of bed, put on a fresh tunic and

went to see what was for breakfast. Aunt Esther was at the table serving Uncle Solomon and Father hot bread and honey. She smiled at him as if she knew something wonderful had taken place. He sat down by his uncle, and picked up a piece of bread and smeared it with honey.

"Benjamin, now that Passover has ended, your aunt and I will be returning to Tiberias. Would you like to go with us?"

"I don't know," Benjamin said, setting the bread down on the table. "Why do you ask?"

"I think it would be wise for you to leave Jerusalem for a while," Father said. "If the Romans find out you have seen Jesus, who knows what might happen?"

"If you come with us, you can see where your Grandfather was born," Aunt Esther said, wiping her hands on her apron. "It's been five years since your cousins were here. They would be thrilled to have you visit them."

"Rueben and Asher can show you how to fish. And you can study the Torah with Isaac," Uncle Solomon said.

Benjamin didn't know what to do. If he left, how could he call on the Holy Spirit for guidance? "Father, I...I..."

"What is it, Benjamin?"

Then the words Jesus spoke about the Holy Spirit being with him always, no matter where he went, flashed in his mind. "Never mind, Father, it's nothing."

"The trip will be good for you," Grandfather said. "There will be many remarkable sights to see."

"But if I go, you'll have to work alone."

"Your father can help. When he was a boy, he was very handy at trimming branches."

"That is right," Father said, nodding.

"Are you sure you can still climb trees?" Benjamin laughed as he pictured his father perched on the limb of an olive tree in his long robe.

His father laughed too. "I think you would be surprised at how capable I still am at scrambling up trees."

"It's settled then," Aunt Esther said. "You'll go back with us."

Uncle Solomon was smearing some bread with honey. "There's a caravan of pilgrims leaving tomorrow. They'll gather in the morning outside the Golden Gate near Mount Mariah. Traveling with them, we'll be sure to have a safe trip. Bandits never bother large caravans."

"Bandits?" Benjamin asked enthusiastically.

"No need to be concerned," Uncle Solomon reassured him. "We've never encountered any in our travels."

"I'm not worried, Uncle. To come face-to-face with one would be exciting."

"Don't even think about it." Aunt Esther shook her finger at Benjamin.

"Son, when you return home, Isaac will join you. Grandfather can use his help harvesting the olives. And when that is finished, the two of you will have plenty of time to study the Torah, since you both want to be rabbis."

"I don't want to be a rabbi any longer." The words slipped out before Benjamin could stop them.

"What do you mean?" Father asked, his eyebrows knitted together into a frown.

Benjamin wished he could take the words back, but it was too late. He shrugged. "So much has happened. My mind is full of questions. I'm not clear about a lot of things."

Father placed his hand on Benjamin's shoulder. "Son, perhaps this time away will help you discover the answers you seek."

SIXTEEN

JOURNEY TO GALILEE

The next morning after breakfast, Benjamin and Uncle Solomon loaded the cart with fresh straw. They piled bundles of firewood and their bedrolls on top.

Aunt Ester brought out a blanket and laid it over a portion of the straw. Next, she placed cloth packs in the cart that had flatbread, dried fish, dried apples, figs, olives, and nuts wrapped inside. She had also packed herbs for dressing wounds, and remedies for indigestion.

Uncle Solomon handed Benjamin a harness. "Here, it's time to hitch up Moshe."

Taking the leather halter, Benjamin went over and gripped the donkey's mane. He tried to slip the bridle over its broad nose, but Moshe yanked away and brayed loudly. "Stand still," Benjamin commanded.

"Let me show you how to win him over," Uncle Solomon said. He rubbed Moshe's head, and scratched behind the animal's ear. Moshe nuzzled his wet nose against the side of Uncle's neck. "Treat him like this, and he's as gentle as a kitten."

"He's a gentle kitten for you. For me, he's still a stubborn old mule."

Uncle laughed. "He's quiet now. Quick, slip the harness on." As soon as Benjamin did, Moshe brayed and bumped him hard in the chest. "See, he hates me."

"No, he just wants to have his own way. After you've handled him a while, he'll get used to you. You'll soon be the best of friends."

Benjamin shook his head. "Never!"

Uncle Solomon chuckled and attached a rope to the harness. "Moshe, you better behave yourself," he said, stroking the animal's neck. "We have a lengthy journey ahead."

Father came from the house carrying a brown cape. He draped it across Benjamin's shoulders. "You will want this to keep the sun off during the day and the chill off at night."

The cape was the one Benjamin's mother had made for him when he turned thirteen. Her scent still clung to the garment. "I miss her," he said softly.

Father pulled Benjamin into his arms and kissed his cheek. "I miss her too."

Benjamin's throat tightened. He couldn't remember the last time his father had kissed him.

Grandfather came from behind the house with two bulging leather water pouches. He heaved them into the cart. "You'll be glad to have these when the sun's at its hottest. Solomon, be sure to pace yourself. You're not as young as you used to be."

"I can still run circles around you Jacob," Uncle Solomon said, laughingly.

Aunt Esther came outside. Her hair, neatly braided and wrapped around the crown of her head, peeked out from under her headscarf. "I'm ready," she said, sniffling. She gave hugs to Grandfather and Father. "Don't worry, Samuel. We'll take good care of your son." Tears wet her cheeks.

Grandfather grabbed Benjamin into a hug. "Stay on the path," he whispered. "Don't wander off alone. Wild animals are always looking for their next meal, and they're not particular about what they eat."

"Don't worry. I'll stick close to the caravan." Benjamin playfully tugged his grandfather's beard.

Aunt Esther climbed into the cart and rearranged the cloth packs, wood bundles, and bedrolls before she sat down on the blanket.

Uncle Solomon gripped Moshe's rein, gave a yank, and the cart surged forward. Benjamin fell in behind. The wheels creaked loudly under the heavy weight. Just as they reached the edge of the olive grove, Benjamin heard Grandfather call, "Don't forget, I want you home for the harvest."

He turned and waved. Father and Grandfather were standing side by side, their arms linked.

Up ahead, Daniel and Rachel were working in their mother's vegetable garden. Daniel leaned on a hoe while Rachel, on her hands and knees, pulled weeds.

"Uncle, may I say good-bye to my friends?"

"Don't be long."

"Daniel, Rachel," Benjamin shouted as he ran toward them.

Daniel waved the hoe. Rachel got up and wiped her hands on her apron.

"I'm going to Tiberias with my aunt and uncle. But I'll be back in time for the harvest."

Daniel dug the sharp edge of the hoe into the ground. "I wish I could go with you. Why am I left behind to do women's work?"

"I'll be back before you miss me."

"That's not true. I'll – I mean, we'll miss you." Rachel blushed and lowered her eyes.

Benjamin face felt hot and his throat went dry. Still he choked out the words, "I'll miss you, too. Both of you," he said quickly. Then he punched Daniel's arm. "Don't get into any fights without me."

"I won't."

"I'd better get going." He ran to catch up with the cart.

As he approached it, Aunt Esther smiled. "Benjamin, there's a sparkle in your eyes."

He ignored his aunt's comment and looked over his shoulder at Rachel. She waved to him. As he lifted his arm to wave to her, it struck him that maybe the Holy Spirit had visited Daniel and Rachel, too. After all, they had been in the upper room. Since he couldn't go back to find out, he'd have to wait until he returned.

"Look!" Uncle Solomon pointed up the road toward the Golden Gate situated on the distant wall of the city. "There's the caravan that we'll travel with. Let's hurry." He tugged Moshe's rein. "They're beginning to move out. We don't want to be at the back of the caravan, it's too dusty."

Up ahead a group of fifty or more pilgrims began heading down the road, going northeast away from the city toward Jericho. Oxen and donkeys pulled carts that creaked and groaned under cumbersome loads. Men led camels weighed down with purchases made during the festival. Their wives walked beside them while their children played games of tag.

They hurried to join the travelers. Many people were discussing the events of Passover, but no one spoke of Jesus' death or the empty tomb.

Rabbis could be heard arguing the religious laws. Dust kicked up under the travelers' feet and clung to everything. The caravan moved steadily down the road like a swarm of locusts.

There were people from Ephraim, Sychar, and Cana to name just a few cities. Men talked about their trades with such passion that Benjamin could feel the intense heat of a blacksmith's fire, smell the wood shavings of a carpenter's shop, and taste the fresh fish caught by a skilled fisherman.

Aunt Esther chatted with any woman who ventured close to the cart. Soon she grew tired of talking. She curled up on the blanket and fell asleep.

Benjamin placed the hood of his cape over his head to block out the intense heat of the sun. The muscles in his legs ached. He longed to rub the dull pain away, but Uncle Solomon never stopped long enough to give him a chance.

Pebbles worked their way into Benjamin's sandals

and wedged between his toes. They burned like hot embers. He dug them out, but new ones took their place. Soon he gave up. How did pilgrims do this every Passover? Their faith must give them the strength for the long journey.

Later, the sun was directly overhead and the caravan pulled off the road. Aunt Esther sat up, rubbing her eyes. "Solomon, dear, are we stopping?"

"Yes, Esther." He led Moshe to a shady place next to a large tree.

Once the cart halted, Aunt Esther handed a cloth pack and water pouch to Benjamin. "Here, put these under the shade tree."

Other families in the caravan were already spreading their blankets and setting out food.

Uncle Solomon dug a hole and poured water in it for Moshe. Aunt Esther laid a white cloth under the tree. She sat and unpacked bread, dried apples, and a jar of honey. "Benjamin, sit here next to me." She patted the ground.

Uncle Solomon joined them and prayed, "Lord, bless this food that it may nourish and strengthen our bodies for the journey ahead." He tore off a piece of bread and passed the rest to Benjamin. "We're making good time. If we continue at this pace, we'll bypass Jericho before nightfall and camp with the others."

Aunt Esther passed Benjamin the water pouch, and he drank until water spilled from the sides of his mouth. Quickly wiping his face with his sleeve, he said, "Uncle, my legs hurt. How can you keep going?"

"You'll get used to it. By the end of the journey,

your legs will bulge with muscles like mine." He laughed and brushed some crumbs from the front of his robe. "Some of the others are finished eating and are already packing up. We'd better hurry. We don't want to be left behind."

They re-packed the cart and started down the dusty road. The caravan moved steadily along. The children, who ran around at the start of the day, now rode on their father's shoulders, or in carts. Benjamin tried to lengthen his stride to keep up with his uncle's quick steps. Aunt Esther, riding in the cart, nodded off again.

The Judean hills surrounded them, and the fragrance from cedar trees filled the air. Yellow crown daisies blanketed the fields. From a rocky ledge overhead, an eagle took flight. Benjamin pointed to the bird. "I wish I could fly like that."

"Men don't fly, they walk. That's why God gave us two legs instead of wings."

"Uncle, see what power and freedom it has as it circles around."

"I see, but he circles for a reason. Watch."

The eagle swooped down and snatched up a large snake that was sunning itself on a boulder by the side of the road. The long talons grasped the wriggling snake as it fought to get free. The eagle's claws crushed its prey and the snake stopped twisting.

"They have power, but they use their power in a menacing way," Uncle Solomon said.

The eagle stroked the air with its broad wings. Benjamin watched it until it soared out of sight. "I'd still like to have the freedom to fly," he said.

"Yes, yes, that would be nice, but impossible." Uncle Solomon wiped sweat from his bald head. "Benjamin, fetch me some water, and don't disturb your aunt."

At the back of the cart, Benjamin searched for a water pouch. "You!" An anguished voice from behind him said. "You were at Golgotha when they led Jesus to his death."

Benjamin spun around to face a man with dirty, tangled hair and a disheveled beard. The tormented eyes that stared out of the man's shabby looking face belonged to the renegade, Barabbas. Benjamin tried to walk away from him, but Barabbas latched on to his arm. "I need to talk with you."

"Leave me alone." Benjamin tried to shake off the man's hand.

"Let me talk to you. I want you to explain—"

"What's going on?" Uncle Solomon said as he halted Moshe. "Take your hands off my nephew."

Barabbas released Benjamin's arm. "I was just talking with the boy."

"Well, move on."

Barabbas leaned forward and whispered, "I don't want to hurt you. I just need some answers." He backed away and disappeared into a group of pilgrims at the rear of the caravan.

SEVENTEEN

NIGHTFALL

Before sunset, the caravan's carts, one by one, pulled off the road. The pilgrims began to prepare their campsites for the night.

Uncle Solomon brought Moshe to a halt by a large grassy field where many families were already setting up and starting fires.

"Where are we?" Aunt Esther asked, sitting up in the cart and rubbing her eyes.

"A few miles north of Jericho," Uncle Solomon said. "I'll unhitch Moshe and feed him. Benjamin, you unload the bundles of wood, put them by the level ground away from the cart, and fetch some kindling so I can start a fire."

Benjamin stacked the wood where Uncle Solomon had told him. Wandering to the edge of the campsites where other boys were gathering twigs, he piled his arms with small, dead branches. As he made his way back to camp, dozens of fires were already glowing in the twilight.

"Is this enough?" Benjamin asked, dropping the sticks next to where his uncle had dug a hole and lined the edge with stones.

"More than enough," Uncle Solomon answered while he placed some dry grass into the pit. Taking a piece of flint from a small leather bag, he hit it on the blade of his knife. Sparks flew and landed on the grass. He blew into the smoldering tinder until it burst into flames. He added the kindling and when that was ablaze, he added a few bigger pieces.

Benjamin stepped back. "How did you do that so fast?"

"Practice, Benjamin, practice."

Aunt Esther laid a white cloth on the ground. She set flatbread, dried fish, and plump figs next to a pouch of water. "Everything's ready," she announced.

Once they were all seated, Uncle Solomon said a prayer, asking the Lord to bless their food. During the meal, Benjamin's head bobbed.

Aunt Esther nudged his arm. "Don't fall asleep before you've finished eating."

"Tomorrow, we'll bypass Ephraim and journey to the Jordan River to replenish our water," Uncle Solomon said. "Now that we have our walking legs, we can travel farther and faster than we did today."

Benjamin flinched as he rubbed the sore muscles in his legs. Would he ever develop the strength to keep up?

The sun sank behind the hills, and before long the yellow glow of the moon filled the blue-black sky. Fires blazed brightly at the campsites.

Aunt Esther wrapped up the leftovers. "Give me a hand putting the cloth packs by the fire, Benjamin. The flames will keep the jackals away from our food."

"After you help your aunt, get the bedrolls and unroll them near the fire," Uncle Solomon directed. "But not too close."

Benjamin did as he was told. The night air had grown cold. Uncle Solomon placed more wood on the glowing flames. "Don't stray beyond the campsite," he said. "Wild animals roam at night looking for a kill."

Benjamin nodded and stretched out on his bedroll. He watched while his aunt and uncle crawled under their blankets. The stars blinked brightly in the sky like lightning bugs on a warm summer night. He yawned and yanked his cloak over his head. Within minutes, he was fast asleep.

In the middle of the night, Benjamin awoke needing to relieve himself. Hot embers still glowed in many of the fires. He tossed off his cloak, got up, and made his way to the far end of the camp. Looking for a private place, he followed the moonlit path that led beyond the campsite. Benjamin relieved himself behind a clump of bushes. As he stepped back onto the dark path, a large hand clamped over his mouth.

"Don't be afraid." The voice was raspy and the hand calloused. Thick fingers pressed into Benjamin's cheeks. "I'm going to take my hand away. Don't cry out. I won't hurt you."

Benjamin, his heart pounding, nodded. The hand loosened and turned him around. Benjamin stood face to face with the criminal, Barabbas. The man's tormented eyes now seemed full of regret, but he continued to hang onto Benjamin's arms.

"You were there when the people called for Jesus to be crucified. Why did they do that? He was innocent. I killed many in the uprising, yet they set me free."

Benjamin stared at Barabbas and tried not to show fear. "The Jewish leaders freed you because they didn't want Jesus alive. He was a threat to everything they believed in."

"You kept calling his name to set him free. Are you one of his followers?"

"I'm not. But now that I know He's the Messiah, I want to become one."

"The Messiah? No, Jesus was a rabbi, and now he's dead. The Messiah is still to come. He'll help us drive the Romans from our land."

"You're wrong."

Barabbas relaxed his hold. "What do you mean?"

Benjamin could have easily pulled away and run back to the camp. But he didn't because any fear he had felt earlier was gone. Instead, he said boldly, "Jesus is alive."

"That's impossible. With my own eyes I saw him die on Calvary."

"No, He lives."

"You lie."

"I'm telling the truth. I spoke with Him."

Barabbas shook his head. "No one comes back from the dead."

"Jesus brought His friend, Lazarus, back to life and Jesus is—"

"He's alive? You're certain?"

"Yes, He's come back to—"

"If it's true and if Jesus is the Messiah returned from the dead to drive the Romans out of Jerusalem, I need to find him and join the fight." Barabbas let go of Benjamin's arms and ran off, disappearing into the dark of night.

Benjamin had wanted to tell Barabbas that he didn't think Jesus came back to lead the Jews in a battle against the Romans. Jesus was the Messiah, but He was not what the people expected.

Not wanting to worry his aunt and uncle, he decided to keep this encounter to himself. He quickly returned to his bedroll and tried to sleep.

EIGHTEEN

GASPAR

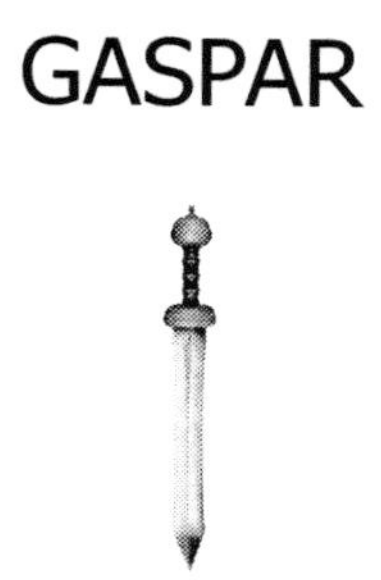

The next morning, the pilgrims packed up their gear. Fires were snuffed out, animals were harnessed, and carts were pulled out onto the road.

After a night of restlessness, Benjamin trudged behind his uncle's cart, struggling to stay awake. Unable to sleep because of his run-in with Barabbas, he knew he'd never be able to keep up with his uncle's quick strides.

The dusty air, stirred up by carts' wheels, travelers' feet and animals' hooves, made Benjamin's lungs burn, and he started to cough.

"Dear boy, you look ill. Come, ride with me a while." Aunt Esther patted the place next to her.

"I'm all right, Auntie."

"You look as if you can't take another step. Solomon, stop the cart. The boy is exhausted. He needs to rest."

Uncle Solomon shook his head as he led Moshe

to the side of the road. "Don't argue with your aunt. You'll never win."

"Dear boy, we don't want you sick."

"You heard her. If we continue at this pace, it will be nightfall before we reach the Jordan River. You'd better ride."

Benjamin shrugged and climbed in beside Aunt Esther. "I'm really not tired, but if you insist..."

Inside the cart, he laid his head on a bedroll and immediately fell asleep.

When he woke, the heat of the sun was directly overhead. He squinted and sat up. Looking around he saw that their cart had fallen a short distance behind the caravan. Aunt Esther was no longer next to him.

"It's about time you woke up." Uncle Solomon laughed, looking over his shoulder. "I thought you'd sleep all day."

"Don't scold the boy. He needed to rest," Aunt Esther said as she walked slowly alongside Uncle Solomon.

Benjamin jumped down from the cart and fell into step between them.

"My arms are sore," Uncle Solomon said. "Will you take the reins awhile?"

Benjamin nodded and took the rope. Moshe bumped her nose against his shoulder, knocking him off balance. "Stop that!" He grabbed the donkey's mane to steady himself. The hairs were stiff and coarse.

"She's still a bit temperamental when it comes to

someone new. If you rub behind her ear, she'll settle down."

Benjamin scratched Moshe's ear, and the animal immediately sprayed him with a big wet snort.

"See, she likes you."

Swiping his sleeve across his face, Benjamin grinned. "It's not me she likes, it's the scratching."

All of a sudden, a camel carrying a dark-skinned young man raced along the outer edge of the road. Dirt and rocks flew in every direction.

"He had better slow down before he hurts himself or someone else," Aunt Esther said, shaking her head.

A white cloak, trimmed with purple cording, billowed behind the rider. The matching headdress that was tightly wrapped around his head was different than any Benjamin had seen before. "Uncle, where do you think he's from?"

"The dark skin tells me he might be from Egypt or Ethiopia. With such a fine blanket and decorative saddle, he must be a person of wealth."

Aunt Esther brushed dirt from her clothes. "Enough about that ruffian. I'm more interested in what your father told us. He said that you have memorized the story of Joshua at the wall of Jericho. Is that true?"

"Father encouraged me to learn about our people's history. We used to study together."

"Be a dear boy and recite it for us. It will help pass the time now that the caravan is ahead of us, and there's no one to talk to."

Benjamin hesitated.

"You better do what she asks, or she'll keep pestering you."

"All right." Benjamin cleared his throat. "As you know, Auntie, Jericho is the oldest city in Judah. It was the land promised to the Israelites by God. Moses led them out of slavery in Egypt and into the desert where they wandered for forty years. Moses died before he arrived at the Promised Land, and Joshua was told by God to lead the Jews across the Jordan River into Jericho and to capture the city."

Aunt Esther sighed. "Just think, Moses wandered for forty years and never entered the Promised Land. Such a shame. He was almost always faithful."

"Yes, Yes," Uncle Solomon said. "Now, let Benjamin continue."

"Auntie, can you imagine the fear in the people of Jericho when they saw the army of thousands marching toward their city? I wish I could've been there."

Aunt Esther's eyes widened. "I would have been afraid."

"Esther, let the boy finish." Uncle Solomon nodded at Benjamin.

"As you can imagine, with such an enormous wall surrounding the city, the people felt fairly secure. Still, they ran to close and lock the gates." Benjamin paused and looked at Aunt Esther.

"Go on," she said, smiling.

Benjamin glanced away to keep from laughing. He

took a deep breath and started again. "You see Auntie, God directed Joshua to march his army around the wall for seven days. The priests were to follow and carry the Holy Ark. The first six days they marched around the walls in complete silence. On the seventh day they went around the wall seven times. At the end of the seventh time, the priest blew the ram's horn."

"You mean the shofar, dear boy?"

Uncle Solomon sighed. "Of course he means the shofar."

Benjamin grinned and continued, "After the priest blew the shofar, the people shouted with all their might, and to their amazement, the wall crumbled."

"Do you think Joshua believed the wall would actually give way?" Aunt Esther asked.

Uncle Solomon rubbed his forehead. "Esther, Joshua must have trusted in what the Lord told him. The important thing is – he obeyed."

"Yes, and once the walls fell, Joshua's great army captured the city," Benjamin added quickly. "Auntie, that's all I've committed to memory."

Aunt Esther applauded. "You're a wonderful storyteller!"

"Esther, it's more than a story. It's part of our history."

"I know, I know. I'm thirsty. Can we stop?"

"No wonder your throat's dry, Esther. With all the interrupting you've done, you should be as parched as the desert during a drought." Uncle Solomon and Benjamin both laughed.

Aunt Esther ignored them. She pointed to some palm trees at the side of the road. "We can sit over there and refresh ourselves."

Uncle Solomon took the reins from Benjamin. "We can't stop long or we'll lose sight of the caravan." He led Moshe over to the trees.

Benjamin lifted a water pouch from the cart, and as he handed it to Aunt Esther, he saw something round and thorny hanging on a cactus. "Auntie, what's that?"

"It's Sabrah, a fruit that has sweet meaty pulp and juice inside. Just thinking about it makes my mouth water. Pick some for us."

Benjamin walked over to the cactus. Reaching for the fruit, he spotted a ravine directly in front of him. At the bottom of it was a crumpled white cloak trimmed with a purple cord. Feet and legs stuck out from underneath it.

"Uncle, come quick!" Benjamin hollered. He hopped down into the ditch and pulled the garment back. The young man, who had raced by on the camel earlier, lay there unconscious. His turban was next to him, and he had a large lump on his forehead.

Uncle Solomon appeared at the top of the incline. "Are you all right, Benjamin?"

"Yes, but he's not."

Uncle Solomon skidded down next to Benjamin. He examined the young man's head, and then shouted, "Esther, bring me some water."

Aunt Esther hurried over with a water pouch and

handed it down to Uncle Solomon. "My goodness! Is he alive?"

"He's still breathing."

"What do you think happened?" Benjamin asked.

"I don't know." Uncle Solomon placed the pouch to the young man's lips. A trickle of water flowed out.

The young man's eyes fluttered open. He sat up quickly, knocking the pouch away. Grabbing the top of his head with both hands, he let out a groan. "Who are you?" he mumbled.

"We're travelers going home to Tiberias from Jerusalem. We stopped for a drink of water and my nephew spotted you lying here in a heap. What happened?"

"The last thing I remember was getting off my camel." He looked at Aunt Esther and lowered his voice, "I had to relieve myself. Someone grabbed me from behind and hit me with something hard." He quickly searched his pockets. "They've taken my money, and where's Ade?"

Benjamin glanced around. "Who's Ade?"

"My camel."

"It must have run off."

"He'd never do that."

"Whoever attacked you must have taken him too."

The young man reached into the top of his boot and withdrew a dagger. "Well, they didn't get this. They caught me by surprise. Otherwise I would have used it on them."

"Put that away," Aunt Esther scolded. "Someone could get hurt."

The young man lowered his eyes and slid the dagger back into his boot.

"Let me clean that bruise for you," Aunt Esther said.

Benjamin grabbed the young man's turban as he and Uncle Solomon helped him out of the ditch.

"Come sit with us while my wife attends to you."

At the cart, Aunt Esther washed the bruise.

"Where are you from?" Benjamin asked.

"Assab, a seaport town in Ethiopia."

"What brings you here?"

"I boarded a ship and sailed up through the Red Sea to the Gulf of Agaba. I landed in Jordan, where I purchased Ade."

"What do they call you?"

"I'm named for my grandfather, Gaspar, a great astronomer."

"Astronomers study the stars," Benjamin said, proud that he recognized the term.

"That's true. Some years back while my grandfather was studying the night sky, he discovered two bright stars that intersected and appeared as one. From his studies, he recognized this as a sign that a new king would be born. He was intrigued and set out with two other astronomers to follow the star that would lead to the infant."

"Did they find him?"

"The star guided them to Bethlehem, to a cave where

they found a baby boy born of poor parents. There was a brilliant aura around the child. Angels sang and shepherds came to give homage. My grandfather believed the infant would one day be a great king. The baby's name was Jesus."

Benjamin gasped. "Are you sure that was his name?"

"Yes, my grandfather always wanted to return to find out what happened to the child. As he aged, he fell ill and couldn't travel. This year he believed that at sixteen I was old enough to make the journey alone, so he sent me in his place."

"Where were you going in such a hurry when you passed us earlier?" Uncle Solomon asked.

"My travels first took me to Bethlehem. People there knew nothing of the child. So I came to Jerusalem, looking for information. I was told that a man they called Jesus, who was born in Bethlehem, was recently hung on a cross like a common criminal. I heard that after his death he was laid to rest in a tomb near a place called Calvary."

Benjamin wanted to tell Gaspar all about Jesus, but the young man wouldn't stop talking.

"I found the tomb, but I was told it was empty. There, I overheard some men talking quietly about Jesus coming back from the dead. At first, I didn't believe it, but they kept whispering about how he appeared to them and told them to meet him at the Sea of Galilee. I decided to go there, too. I wanted to find out if this Jesus was the one my grandfather thought would become King. I was on my way there when I was attacked."

"Jesus is going to be at the Sea of Galilee?" Benjamin trembled with excitement

"That's what I heard. Now, without my camel, I'm afraid Jesus will be gone before I get there."

"We're going to Tiberias, on the Sea of Galilee. Come with us. If Jesus is there we'll find Him. Isn't that right, Uncle?"

"Perhaps," Uncle Solomon said, looking around. "It's getting late. I don't see the caravan. We'd better get back on the road."

"But Solomon, I still need to quench my thirst. And what about the sabrah?"

"Esther, dear, we'll have our water, but the fruit will have to wait for another time."

Gaspar leaned over to Benjamin. "Do you think the men in Jerusalem were telling the truth about meeting Jesus?"

"If Jesus told some of His followers He'd meet them at the Sea of Galilee, He'll be there."

NINETEEN

JORDAN RIVER

Uncle Solomon passed around one of the water pouches. Everyone drank until it was empty. "We'll reach the Jordan later today and fill this back up," he said, setting the pouch in the cart. "We'd better leave. I'd like to catch up with the caravan before it arrives at the river."

"Gaspar, ride with me, at least until your head feels better," Aunt Esther said, climbing into the cart.

"I'd rather walk. It doesn't hurt much anymore." He wrapped his turban loosely on his head and stepped in alongside Benjamin.

Uncle Solomon seized Moshe's reins and started out. Aunt Esther leaned back in the cart and closed her eyes.

As they traveled, Benjamin had many questions that he wanted to ask Gaspar, but Uncle Solomon picked up the pace to a point where conversation was impossible.

The caravan finally came into sight. Some families were veering off the main road and heading down a narrow path.

"Where are they going, Uncle?"

"They're traveling west across the valley to Arimathea. We're going east over the hills with those who are stopping at the Jordan River for water."

Just before they reached the caravan, Benjamin spotted a camel with a familiar decorative saddle next to a nearby hill. A tall, scrawny man stood holding the animal's rein. Close by, two other men appeared to be talking; one wore a shabby cloak and the other was bent with age.

"Gaspar, could that be your camel?" Benjamin gestured toward the three men.

The young Ethiopian shaded his eyes from the sun with both hands. "Yes. It's Ade. They must be the thieves who stole him." Without another word, he headed at a fast pace toward the men.

"Wait for me!" Benjamin said, setting off after him.

"Where are you two going?" Uncle Solomon grabbed for the sleeve of Benjamin's tunic, but missed.

"To get Gaspar's camel," Benjamin said over his shoulder.

As they left the dusty road and headed across the grassy area toward the hill, Gaspar said, "Let's be careful. We don't want to be seen and scare them off."

Benjamin saw that the old man was dropping some coins into the hands of the man with the shabby cloak.

When Gaspar and Benjamin got closer, the man who received the money glanced at them. In a moment of recognition, he grabbed the camel's rein from his cohort and shoved it into the old man's hands. Then he took off running. His partner, seeing him, ran too.

"Stop, thieves!" Gaspar hollered as he pursued them. Benjamin followed right behind.

The men darted into a wide opening in the hillside.

Gaspar and Benjamin raced after them.

In the gray shadows of the cave, it was clear that the thieves had their knives drawn. Gaspar slid his dagger from the top of his boot.

"Don't risk getting yourself killed, Gaspar," Benjamin shouted. "You found Ade. That's enough."

"But they still have my money."

The shabby-cloaked man sneered, "Your friend is wise. The camel's not worth dying for. And we didn't take your money."

"Liars! I'll show you who will die this day." Gaspar lunged forward with his dagger, stabbing wildly in the air.

The men seemed startled. The one man dropped a leather pouch that clinked as it hit the ground. Then the two scurried deeper into the darkness. Gaspar started after them, but Benjamin grabbed his arm. "Remember why we're going to Galilee."

Gaspar shook Benjamin's hand loose. "They don't deserve to get away without paying for their thievery."

"Isn't finding Jesus more important than revenge?"

Gaspar drew a deep breath and nodded. "You're right." He slid his dagger back into the top of his boot, reached over and picked up the leather pouch. Jiggling it, he said, "Sounds like all my money is here. Let's go before I do something I'll regret."

They left the gloominess of the cave and walked into the bright sunlight. Uncle Solomon and Aunt Esther were waiting next to their cart with the old man. His uncle didn't say anything, but he gave Benjamin a harsh look, showing his displeasure at the two of them for running off without considering the worry they would cause.

The old man's hands trembled as he clutched Ade's rein.

Gaspar quickly snatched it away. "Ade is mine. Those bandits stole him."

The lines in the old man's face deepened as if he was going to cry. Aunt Esther touched Gaspar's shoulder. "This is Huram. He didn't steal Ade. He's on his way to Tiberias to be with his wife. While visiting their son she became ill. They sent for Huram to come at once."

The old man let out a long sigh. "I've been traveling for days. When those men asked me if I'd like to buy their camel, I was thankful. My poor feet can walk no farther."

Huram's feet were caked with dirt, and were cracked and bloody. The soles of his sandals were worn thin.

Gaspar stroked Ade's neck gently. Suddenly, he thrust the animal's rein into the old man's hands.

"Here, take him! But when I arrive in Tiberias, I'll find your son's house and get Ade back. You can borrow him. Do you understand?"

Huram thanked Gaspar repeatedly, and gave Gaspar directions to his son's house in Tiberias. Gaspar stared at the ground, his shoulders slumped forward. "Go, before I change my mind. But first, here, some of this money must be yours." Gaspar pulled open his pouch and poured some coins into Huram's free hand.

The old man grabbed Gaspar's hand and kissed it.

Taken by surprise, Gaspar was left staring with his mouth wide open.

Huram smiled a toothless grin and quickly tugged on Ade's rein. The camel knelt while the old man slipped into the saddle. He yanked the rein once more, and Ade lumbered up. With a nudge from Huram's heels, the animal galloped away in a dusty haze.

"Are you all right, Gaspar?" Benjamin asked.

Gaspar, no longer dazed, shrugged. "I couldn't let the elderly gentleman continue to walk on those bloody feet, could I?"

"May the Lord bless you for your kind gesture," Aunt Esther said, patting Gaspar's shoulder.

Gaspar shrugged again, but this time a smile crept across his lips.

Uncle Solomon picked up Moshe's rope. "We should leave. The caravan is well ahead of us."

Aunt Esther lifted another water pouch from the cart and handed it to Uncle Solomon. "We'd better have a drink before we leave, but do it sparingly. This is the last of our water."

As soon as they each had their fill, they headed down the road. The sun overhead was hot, with heat waves rising from the parched ground. They traveled silently at a steady pace, until they caught up to the caravan.

At the banks of the Jordan River, Uncle Solomon pulled the cart up near the riverbed. He handed Benjamin the two leather pouches. "Take these and fill them."

Gaspar reached for one. "I'll help."

They set the pouches on the bank and waded into the river. Cupping their hands, they splashed water on their sweaty faces and drank thirstily. The pouches were then retrieved and filled until they bulged. On shore, Benjamin and Gaspar carried them to the cart and set them inside.

Uncle Solomon was nearby talking with a group of men. Aunt Esther, amid a group of women, pointed toward Benjamin and Gaspar. The women smiled. Benjamin nodded politely.

"I wonder what your Aunt's saying about us."

Benjamin laughed. "I can't imagine."

"I'm surprised your uncle isn't in a hurry now. See how relaxed he is?"

Benjamin looked, but instead of his uncle, he saw a man in a brown hooded robe standing alone by the river. The man must have seen Benjamin at the same time because he started to walk toward them.

"I know that man," Benjamin whispered.

"What man?"

"The one coming this way."

"Who is he?"

"Marcus, a Roman soldier from Jerusalem."

"Why's he wearing a robe, instead of a uniform?"

"I'll explain later."

Marcus stopped in front of Benjamin. "May I talk with you – alone?" His eyes shifted back and forth nervously.

Gaspar looked hesitant.

"It's all right, Gaspar. But don't go far."

Gaspar walked away while Benjamin planted his feet firmly and stared at Marcus. "What do you want?" he asked. Without his uniform, the soldier seemed harmless.

"The day after Jesus was crucified, I deserted my post."

"What does that have to do with me?"

"We soldiers stripped Jesus of his clothes. He told us that we could take everything from him, even his life, but his Father's love could never be taken away. He said, 'God's love overcomes hatred and destroys death.' I never knew that that kind of love existed."

Not knowing what to say, Benjamin remained silent.

"When Jesus said, 'Forgive them, Father, for they know not what they do.' I knew instantly that he forgave me for my part in his death, and for the misery

I caused the Jews. Jesus freed me from my sins. But, I need you to forgive me too."

"What are you talking about?"

Marcus lowered his head. "I was the one who stabbed your mother that day in Jerusalem. It was in the heat of battle. I didn't mean to. The rebel stepped aside and my sword plunged into her."

Benjamin's knees went weak. He wanted to scream at Marcus to stop talking, but the words caught in his throat.

Marcus continued, "I never meant to hurt your mother. Can you forgive me?"

Benjamin's mind reeled. "Never! I can never forgive you!"

"Soldiering was my life. I did what I was trained to do. I can't live like that any longer." Marcus leaned forward and whispered, "If I'm caught, they'll hang me for treason."

Benjamin gritted his teeth. "Why should I care?"

"You're right. Still, I beg you to forgive me!"

He could plead all he wanted; Benjamin was not going to listen. But then he heard the words Jesus spoke during their meeting in the tomb, explaining the difficulty of forgiveness. He rubbed his temples and an image appeared – the dream where his mother told him that it mattered for him to love and be loved and to love and serve God. Benjamin knew it wouldn't be easy. And no matter what he decided to do, it wouldn't bring his mother back.

Benjamin looked into Marcus' eyes and saw tears. He felt a warmth surge though his body. The next words out of his mouth surprised even him. "Marcus, did you hear about the empty tomb and how Jesus appeared to his disciples?"

"I did hear about it before I left the city."

"Well, I've seen Him, and He spoke with me."

"So it's true?"

"Yes, and he told some of his followers that he would meet them at the Sea of Galilee. That's where we're going." Benjamin swallowed hard. "You could come with us."

"If I'm discovered with you, you'll be arrested, too."

"They'd never suspect that you'd be traveling with Jews."

Gaspar approached them. "Benjamin, is anything the matter?"

"Marcus is going to join us on our journey to Galilee."

"Shouldn't you ask your uncle about this first?"

"He's right," Marcus said, nodding.

Benjamin shrugged, but then he hurried to where his uncle stood. "May I speak to you? It's important."

Uncle Solomon excused himself from the group of men. "What is it, Benjamin? You look worried."

"The man with Gaspar, I asked him to travel with us to Tiberias."

"Who is he?" Uncle Solomon was frowning.

"Marcus, a Roman soldier from Jerusalem."

"A Roman soldier? What's he doing here?"

"He's a deserter," Benjamin whispered.

Uncle Solomon scowled. "Get rid of him. He'll cause us nothing but trouble."

"Uncle, please let him come. He needs our help. And when we find Jesus—"

"This is foolishness. If he's with us and the soldiers come, what do you think will happen?"

"But Uncle."

"This man will only use us as a means to escape."

"He didn't ask to travel with us. It was my idea. Don't you understand? Jesus showed us that we must love one another, even our enemies, didn't he?"

There was a long pause, finally his uncle said, "Perhaps you're right, but to take him along—"

"We must do this."

Uncle Solomon rubbed his bald head. "I know I'm going to regret this."

"Auntie would tell us that we'll be blessed if we help him."

"All right Benjamin, I won't argue anymore, but if he comes with us we had better start praying. If we're caught harboring a deserter, the Romans will show us no mercy."

TWENTY

APOSTLES

The caravan of pilgrims settled in for the night along the Jordan River. Flames danced in fires around the campsite. Benjamin's eyes, heavy with sleep, caught a movement next to him. Marcus slid something from under his brown robe. Benjamin squinted. Visible in the moonlight was the handle of Marcus' sword encased in a sheath, and attached to a brass belt. Marcus shoved them under the ground mat that Aunt Esther had given him.

Benjamin wondered why Marcus still had the sword, but this was not the time to ask. He pulled his cloak up to his chin, closed his eyes, and drifted off to sleep. In a dream, he saw himself seize Marcus' sword from its sheath. Raising it high above his head, he swung it downward, crashing the blade against a boulder. The sword shattered into countless pieces.

Benjamin awoke with a start, his sweaty hands

clutched together as if they were still grasping the handle of the sword, but of course they were not.

The camp was quiet except for the sounds of men snoring and embers crackling in smoldering fires. Lying awake, Benjamin thought about the sword, and wondered why Marcus hadn't gotten rid of it. He must have dozed off because the next time he opened his eyes the early morning sun lit up the sky.

Uncle Solomon was standing in front of the fire poking it with a stick to stir the embers. Picking up a piece of wood, he placed it on the fire. It blazed up, and he rubbed his hands together over the heat.

Marcus tilted his head toward Benjamin and whispered, "You risked letting me stay the night. Your uncle is uncomfortable with me being here. I had better leave."

Benjamin pushed his cloak off and bent forward. "You don't have to, unless you feel—"

"Soldiers are coming! Soldiers are coming!" The sound of a woman's shrill voice carried across the campsite.

Gaspar propped himself up on his right elbow and rubbed his eyes. "What's going on?"

A cloud of dust swirled in the air as soldiers on horseback rode into the camp.

Marcus slid his sword, sheath and brass belt from under his ground mat. He shoved them beneath the edge of Benjamin's bedroll. "Take care of these for me."

Benjamin shook his head in protest, but Marcus

ignored him. The soldiers got off their horses. They grabbed some of the pilgrims and shoved them aside, as if they were looking for one particular person.

"Marcus, you'd better hide," Benjamin whispered as he jumped up.

Marcus pulled his hood over his head. "It's too late. I should have left earlier. Don't worry, the soldier leading the troops is my friend, Thaddeus."

Thaddeus strode over to where Uncle Solomon stood near the fire. "We're looking for a soldier who's deserted his post."

"We Jews aren't likely to hide a Roman deserter."

Thaddeus pushed Uncle Solomon aside. He walked over to Benjamin and grabbed his shoulder. "I know you. You're the boy who—"

"Leave him alone, Thaddeus." Marcus leaped up and pulled off his hood. "These people have done nothing. It's me you want. Do what you have to do."

Thaddeus released Benjamin and grabbed Marcus' arm. "I'm under orders. I helped you once, but I can't do it again." He motioned to a soldier standing nearby. "Chain him up!"

Marcus didn't resist. He held out his arms. The soldier wrapped shackles around Marcus' wrists and locked them securely. Thaddeus gripped the iron chain and began to drag Marcus toward the horses.

Benjamin ran up to Thaddeus. "Let him go! He's your friend!"

Thaddeus shoved Benjamin to the ground. He fell

near his bedroll. Sliding his hand under it, he touched the handle of the sword. Could he use it on this soldier? But he remembered how the weapon had plunged into his mother's side. He jerked his hand back as if the handle was on fire and had burned him

Gaspar pulled his dagger from his boot.

"Put that away," Marcus ordered. "I don't want anyone hurt because of me."

Gaspar scowled and slid the dagger back.

Thaddeus mounted his steed. He reached down, grabbed Marcus' chains, and yanked him up behind him. "You can ride with me until we reach Jerusalem. But you'll be dragged along behind the horse when we enter the city. Mount up men."

They rode off in a cloud of dust.

Benjamin got up slowly. "What do you think they'll do to him Uncle?"

"I don't know what they do with deserters," Uncle Solomon said, wringing his hands. "But we did everything we could."

Benjamin shook his head. "I'm sorry I allowed Marcus to put us in danger. I guess I shouldn't have asked him to travel with us, but it seemed like the right thing to do."

"I know," Uncle Solomon said. "Now that it's over, we must not delay any longer. Let's get ready to leave."

Muffled voices could be heard throughout the campsite. Pilgrims were already packing up. Uncle Solomon doused the fire with water.

Not wanting to touch Marcus's sword, but not knowing what else to do, Benjamin rolled all of it up in his bedroll. Gaspar was gathering his things together. Benjamin wondered if he knew about the sword. He carried his bedroll to the cart carefully, checking to see that no one was watching. They were all busy with their own bundles, so he buried his deeply under the straw.

Once the travelers finished packing, they moved out onto the road. They walked in silence, afraid to talk about the incident. The heat of the day became intense as they covered the miles. The sun was directly overhead before the people made their first stop of the day.

Uncle Solomon led Moshe to a place near a palm tree. Four men were seated under it, eating and talking together.

"I know that man," Benjamin said, leaning toward Gaspar. "He's Peter, Jesus' friend."

Peter must have heard his name because he got up and walked over to them. "It's good to see you again, Benjamin. Would you and your family like to join us?"

Benjamin was surprised that Peter remembered him from their time in the upper room. He searched the eyes of his aunt and uncle for approval.

Aunt Esther responded quickly, "I would enjoy visiting with them. What do you think Solomon?"

Uncle Solomon shrugged. "All right, Esther, but don't ask too many questions or we'll be here all day."

Benjamin smiled. He could hardly wait to hear what the men would talk about.

He and Gaspar took a few packs of food from the cart and carried them to the tree where Peter stood with his friends. Aunt Esther put down a white cloth and unwrapped cheese and pieces of fish. Uncle Solomon set out a jug of wine.

"I'd like you to meet my brother, Andrew," Peter said. "And this is John and his brother, James." After that, Benjamin introduced his uncle, aunt, and Gaspar.

Once the introductions ended, Peter lifted his hands in prayer. "Lord, God of Israel, there is no other God like you. We thank you for the food and drink. Bless these travelers with whom we will share this meal."

Peter sat down and the rest followed. He took a loaf of bread, tore off a piece, and handed the rest to Uncle Solomon. "Tell me, where are you headed?"

"We're going home to Tiberias," Uncle Solomon said.

"We're heading there too," James said, nodding.

Uncle Solomon poured wine for the adults. "I'm a fisherman by trade."

"We were fisherman once," John said. "And we plan to go to the Sea of Galilee and fish again."

"You're going to fish?" Benjamin asked. "I thought you were going to..."

"To what?" Peter asked.

Benjamin hesitated. "I-I don't know. I thought maybe you were going there to meet Jesus."

"What makes you think Jesus will be at the Sea of Galilee? What have you heard?"

Gaspar spoke up, "I saw John and James at Jesus' empty tomb in Jerusalem. They were talking in low voices about how Jesus had risen and told them to meet him there."

Peter looked at John and shook his head.

John raised his brow and shrugged. "I'm sorry Peter. We didn't think anyone could hear us."

"That's all right. If he heard you, there must be a reason. Nothing happens without a reason."

Gaspar began to speak again, "My grandfather saw Jesus in Bethlehem shortly after his birth. He believed that Jesus was to become a great King. I wanted to know if it's true. That's why I'm heading for Galilee."

Peter smiled. "Your grandfather was correct. Jesus does have a kingdom, but it's not of this world. And Benjamin, you're right, too. Jesus instructed us to meet Him at the Sea of Galilee. We'll fish there until He comes. As His apostles, we'll follow wherever He leads."

"Apostles?" Benjamin leaned forward. "I thought we were to become His disciples?"

Peter laughed heartily. "A disciple follows Jesus' teachings and passes them on. Apostles are sent out among the people to preach the good news of Jesus' resurrection and the coming of His Kingdom."

"I don't understand," Benjamin said.

Peter laughed again. "Don't worry. You'll learn."

"It looks as though the caravan's heading out," Uncle Solomon said, getting up. "We'd better leave."

"If you'd like, you could travel the rest of the way with us since we're all going to Tiberias," Peter said.

"What a grand idea," Aunt Esther said. "I'd like to hear more about your time with this Jesus."

Uncle Solomon nodded. "It would be a relief to travel with you. We're always losing sight of the caravan and have to rush to catch up with them anyway."

"At the Sea of Galilee, perhaps Benjamin and Gaspar would like to go fishing with us. If it's all right with you, Solomon," Peter said.

"I guess it would be all right. What do you say Esther?"

"Our sons are devoted fishermen, perhaps you could all fish together."

Benjamin was speechless. He could see himself on a boat, the wind in his face, and maybe, just maybe, Jesus would be with them.

TWENTY-ONE

GALILEE

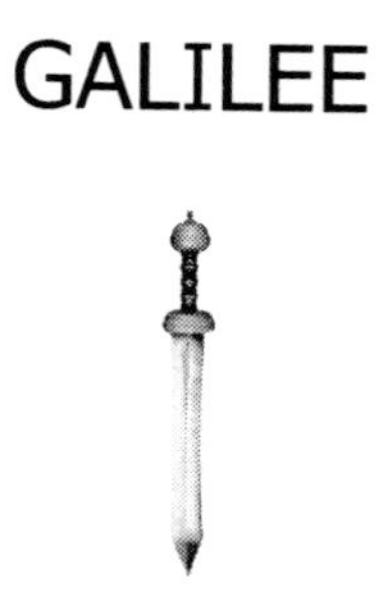

For the next few days of the journey, Benjamin listened to stories about Jesus. While they traveled, he heard about how Peter and the others were called to follow Jesus in His ministry and to become fishers of men.

At night around the campfire, tales were told of the miracles and healings that had taken place. Benjamin was gaining an understanding of what it took to become one of Jesus' disciples. As he slept, the sword he had tucked in his bedroll dug into his back as a constant reminder of his mother's death.

On the morning of the seventh day since their departure from Jerusalem, Mount Tabor appeared in the distance.

From where she sat in the cart, Aunt Esther called out, "Look, the fields are full of wild flowers. I wonder how many I can name?" Uncle Solomon sniffed the air. "You'd better be quick about it because it smells like rain."

Peter studied the dark clouds moving in from the southwest. "You're right, Solomon. We should seek shelter. There's a cave over the next ridge."

As they hurried down the road, the sky turned black. Bolts of lightning stabbed the earth. Aunt Esther bounced around in the cart and she clung to the wooden sides. At the cave, Uncle Solomon led Moshe and the cart into a large opening. The others entered closely behind.

Inside the cave, a pungent odor burned Benjamin's nostrils as he breathed in. Once his eyes adjusted to the darkness, he saw a pile of straw matted down and strewn with bones. Nearby on the ground lay the skulls of small animals. What had happened here?

"Perhaps we've stumbled into the lair of jackals," Peter said. "Those bones are picked clean. Whatever took refuge in this cave ended up as a tasty meal."

"I pray we're not next." Aunt Esther eyed the area suspiciously. "I think I'll stay in the cart."

Peter smiled. "Don't worry. There are enough of us to drive off any animal that might try to attack."

Thunder rumbled in the distance and outside a torrent of rain poured down. "How could you tell a storm was coming, Uncle?" Benjamin asked.

"I could smell it. And my achy old bones felt it."

Peter cleared his throat. "This downpour reminds

me of the time Jesus had us take the boat to the other side of the sea as a storm blew out of the north."

"I've never been in a boat," Benjamin said.

"You'll get your chance soon," Peter said. "But if you think this thunderstorm is wicked, wait until you've experienced a gale on the Sea of Galilee. They come up fast and sweep across the water with a fury." He paused and stared at the ground. He seemed lost in thought.

Benjamin touched Peter's sleeve. "You were telling us about the storm and Jesus."

"So I was. At first the sea was calm. The sail caught a breeze, taking us smoothly away from the shore. Then the wind picked up and the sky turned black. Giant waves tossed us about like a broken branch. As I huddled in the bottom of the boat, I heard my name called. 'Peter, come.' Jesus was walking on the water toward us. He motioned to me. I was amazed and terrified. He held out His hands, and I wanted to go to Him, but I couldn't move. He called my name again, so I got up and stepped out of the boat."

"Did you actually walk on the water?" Benjamin leaned in, not wanting to miss a word.

"As I walked toward Him, I felt no fear. Then I glanced down. The waves crashed against my legs. I had taken my eyes off Jesus for a moment, and I was dragged under. Jesus seized my arm and pulled me up, saying, 'If you have faith and stay focused on me,

Peter, you will never drown, but you will do wonderful things.' He held onto me until I was back in the boat."

Everyone stared at Peter.

Benjamin gulped hard. "When we go fishing, I hope we don't run into such a storm. I don't know how to swim."

"Look, it's stopped raining as quickly as it started," Uncle Solomon said as he stood near the cave's opening. "We had better be on our way." He took Moshe's rein and led the animal, along with Aunt Esther in the cart, through the puddles that had formed outside the cave's entrance.

"Be careful," Aunt Esther said, hanging on tightly to the wooden sides.

The others followed along, sloshing through murky puddles until they reached the road. Cool, wet mud squished into Benjamin's sandals and between his toes.

Then the sun broke through the clouds. Their clothes dried as they trekked along, mile after mile, enjoying the warmth.

At dusk, the sun slipped toward the horizon. A winding path going upward lay before them. Shades of gray slowly surrounded them as they climbed to the top of the ridge. Uncle Solomon halted Moshe and breathed deeply. "Can you smell that?" he asked.

Aunt Esther got out of the cart and stood next to him. "It smells like the sea water of Galilee. We're almost home."

From the top of the ridge, Benjamin saw a large

body of water shimmering in the moonlight. Bonfires dotted the shore.

"This is quite a sight,' Gaspar said.

As they made their way down the bumpy trail, sounds of men talking and laughing reached them.

Peter stopped by a pile of rocks along the shoreline. "We're going to look for our boat. Friends used it while we were gone. It can't be far." He spoke quietly to Uncle Solomon. Then he turned to Benjamin. "We'll meet you and Gaspar here the day after tomorrow to take you fishing before the Sabbath."

As soon as the Apostles said their goodbyes, they headed down the beach.

Benjamin and Gaspar stepped into the water. The yellow beams of moonlight rippled across the sea. Benjamin bent down and splashed the cool wetness on his face, washing off the day's dust. Cupping his hands, he took a long drink.

Behind him, he heard Aunt Esther call out, "Reuben, Asher, Isaac - you're here!"

Benjamin looked over to see Aunt Esther laughing and crying, engulfed in the arms of three grown men.

He waded ashore. "Gaspar, come meet my cousins."

"No, you take time alone with them first."

"Come, Benjamin." Aunt Esther motioned for him. "Do you recognize your cousins?"

"We were about to set sail when we saw Father leading Moshe and the cart down the beach," Reuben said, smiling.

Since the last time Benjamin had seen them, Reuben's black beard had grown thicker and his body was now stockier; Asher's red hair was bushier and his muscular arms bulged; and Isaac was now taller and leaner than both his older brothers.

Reuben patted Benjamin on the back. "It's been a while. You've grown."

Benjamin smiled. "So have you, and so has your beard."

Reuben laughed and tugged at it. "If you eat enough fresh fish, some day you'll have one as thick as mine."

Isaac stood behind Reuben. "I'm glad you came. Now I have someone to study the Torah with. My brothers have little interest in it."

Asher scooped Benjamin into a bear hug. "There'll be plenty of time for studying later. First we'll teach our cousin to fish."

"Father, the fish are scarce," Reuben said. "We drag our nets for hours and only catch a few."

"Why is that?" Uncle Solomon asked.

"We don't know," Asher answered. "It's as if all the fish have been washed downstream into the Jordan River and are ending up at the Dead Sea."

"That's hard to believe." Uncle Solomon rubbed his bald head.

"Come with us tonight. See for yourself," Reuben said.

Aunt Esther's hands were on her hips. "No one will go fishing tonight."

"But, Mother, evenings are the only time we've been able to catch anything," Asher said, frowning. "Even if it's only a few, we must go out and try, otherwise we'll starve."

"There'll be no starving as long as I'm here to cook for you," Aunt Esther replied firmly, then added, "If you must fish, go ahead, but your father needs his rest. He'll go with you tomorrow. Tonight he'll come home with me. What do you say, Solomon?"

"You're right as always, Esther."

"I'll go home, too," Isaac said. "I'm in everybody's way on the boat."

"May Benjamin come with us?" Asher asked.

Uncle Solomon rubbed his eyes. "It's been a long day. He must be tired."

"I'm wide awake, Uncle. Please let me go!" Benjamin felt excited and ready to try anything.

"All right, Benjamin will fish, and I will sleep."

"Wait. I've forgotten someone." Benjamin scanned the water for Gaspar. His friend stood alone on the shore. "Gaspar, come, I want you to meet my cousins."

While his cousins were introducing themselves and patting Gaspar on the back in welcome, Benjamin remembered the sword that was hidden in his bedroll in the cart.

As they continued to exchange pleasantries, Benjamin, now under the cover of darkness, edged his way to the back of the cart and slid the brass belt with the attached sheath and sword out of his bedroll.

He shoved it behind a pile of rocks near the water's edge. Leaving it there, he slipped back to where his uncle stood, yawning and holding Moshe's rein.

"We'll see you at home," Aunt Esther said. "I'll have breakfast waiting for you in the morning."

Isaac led her to the back of the cart and helped her climb in. "Finally, we won't have to eat our own cooking," he said, grinning.

As Uncle Solomon led Moshe down the beach with Isaac at his side, Aunt Esther called and waved, "May you have an abundant catch."

Benjamin and Gaspar waved to her as they trailed behind Reuben and Asher along the beach. Fires that had earlier burned brightly were now out; the men attending them had gone home.

Asher placed a muscular arm across Benjamin's shoulders. "There's nothing like the sea at night. With the moon overhead, the boat beneath your feet, the sail flapping in the breeze, and the wind in your face, it makes you glad to be alive."

"Benjamin, Gaspar, have you ever fished before?" Reuben asked.

"No," they said in unison.

Asher laughed heartily. "Well, Reuben, we'll have to show them how we Galilean fishermen net the big ones."

TWENTY-TWO

FISHERMEN

The moon lit up the night sky, and moonlight shone brightly on a small wooden boat that rested partly in the water along the shoreline and partly in the sand on the beach. A wooden pole rose out of the center and had a white sail lashed to its crossbar.

Benjamin stood behind his cousins on the shore. Gaspar was next to him.

"Is that your boat?" Benjamin asked, gulping down his fear. Not knowing how to swim made him wonder if the slight craft was really safe.

"She's a beauty isn't she?" Asher said proudly. "She can hold all four of us and a full catch of fish."

"Get in," Rueben said. "Asher and I will push it out once you're on board."

Benjamin and Gaspar stepped in cautiously. Rueben and Asher shoved the boat out until it was afloat. When they jumped aboard, it bobbed up and down and rocked from side to side.

Benjamin's stomach churned, and he felt queasy. He and Gaspar crouched in the bow of the boat near some straw baskets and a few circular nets.

Reuben lifted a pair of oars from the bottom of the boat, and after sitting down, he started to row. Once they were away from the shoreline, he brought in the oars. Pulling up the crossbar, he unlashed the sail.

A steady wind pushed them farther out into the night sea. When they were far enough out, Reuben dropped the sail. Using the oars, he steadied the boat.

Asher picked up a net. "We use these cast nets to catch fish," he said. "Keep your eye on me while I show you how to use one. Once you see how it's done, you can each give it a try."

He tied the rope that was attached to the net around his waist. He folded the net over one arm. As he cast it out, it soared over the water and landed on the surface. Heavy weights fastened to the bottom edge caused it to sink a bit.

Benjamin watched, wide-eyed. Would he be able to lift a net and fling it as easily?

After a while, Asher yanked on the rope and the circle closed. He pulled the net into the boat, but there were no fish inside.

"What will you do now?" Gaspar asked.

"I'll keep casting until I catch something. Ready to try?"

Gaspar leaped up, grabbed a net, and cast it out. It landed perfectly. Benjamin got up slowly, trying not to rock the boat. He picked up a net and attempted to do as Asher had instructed. But as he threw it, his net twisted and dropped on the water in a tangled mess.

Embarrassed, he yanked the net back into the boat. He quickly straightened it out and tried again. This time it landed on top of Gaspar's net.

"Sorry," he said, through clenched teeth. How could he be so awkward?

Asher patted him on the back. "Don't worry. You'll get the hang of it."

The two nets were pulled in and untangled. Gaspar once again cast his out with ease, as did Asher. Benjamin held his breath as he let his sail. It soared over the water and dropped gracefully between Gaspar's and Asher's nets. He heaved a sigh of relief.

They cast their nets again and again, but each time they pulled them in, they were empty.

"Don't give up," Asher said. "Maybe the next time we'll haul in a full catch of fish."

A brisk wind suddenly blew in from the north and stirred up the water. Whitecaps began to form and they grew in intensity. Waves slapped against the sides of the boat, pitching it about like a broken twig.

"Hold on, there's a gale blowing," Reuben called. "Pull in your nets. We don't want to lose them."

Asher hauled his into the boat. "Take the rope off your waist and sit on the nets. We don't want them to wash overboard, but if they do, we don't want you going over with them."

Once the nets were secure, Reuben brought in the oars. "The wind's strong. The sail will tear if I try to raise it. We'll have to ride it out."

Reuben and Asher huddled in the bottom of the boat near the mast. Benjamin and Gaspar crouched on their nets in the bow.

A large wave hit broadside, soaking everyone.

Gaspar grinned as water streamed down his face. "What a storm!"

Benjamin nodded in agreement but couldn't stop his teeth from chattering.

A giant swell swamped the boat. Benjamin ducked his head and when he looked up, Gaspar was gone. Benjamin, cold and wet, trembled. He crawled over to the side. Gaspar was thrashing about in the water. A giant wave crashed over him and dragged him under.

Without a moment to lose, Benjamin grabbed the net he was sitting on and tied the piece of rope around his waist. Gaspar surfaced, gasping for air. Benjamin threw the net to him, but it fell short.

Another wave swamped Gaspar. Benjamin yanked the net in and leaned out as far as he could. He tossed it once more. This time Gaspar caught it and hung on.

Benjamin yanked the net in with all his might until he could grasp Gaspar's hand. He tried to lift Gaspar into the boat, but the weight was too much for him. He toppled overboard, plunging into the sea along with his friend.

Waves dragged him under. He began to kick frantically.

He broke through the surface, gasping for air. Water blurred his eyes and ran down his face. In front of him, the outline of the edge of the boat rose and fell. He grabbed it and hung on.

The rope was still wrapped around his waist, and Gaspar was still clinging to the end of the netting.

Benjamin kept kicking with all his might. As he looked up, Reuben and Asher were leaning out over the side of the boat. "Hang on!" Asher shouted.

He seized Benjamin's arms and with a mighty yank pulled him aboard. Then Reuben and Asher hauled Gaspar in.

Benjamin lay flat in the bottom of the boat, coughing and spitting out water. Gaspar was doing the same.

The wind suddenly shifted to the southwest. The violent pitching of the boat settled into a gentle sway. The storm had subsided as quickly as it had started.

"The Sea of Galilee is unpredictable," Asher said, shaking his head. "It's calm one minute and a tempest the next. We never know what to expect."

"Benjamin, you didn't catch any fish yet, but you caught me," Gaspar said, sitting up. "You saved my life. I thought you said you couldn't swim."

"You don't know how to swim?" Asher asked. His brows were arched.

"No, but it was you and Reuben who really saved us."

Reuben shook his head. "If it hadn't been for your quick thinking, Gaspar would have drowned."

Benjamin sat up and shrugged. "You both would've done the same."

Asher laughed. "I know. But we know how to swim."

Benjamin's face turned hot even though the air was cold. He untied the rope from his waist and tucked the net under his legs.

"We're fortunate we didn't lose any of our gear," Rueben said, pulling up the sail. "There's still time to catch some fish. Let's head toward shore."

As they came closer to the shoreline, the moon cast its light on another boat in the water. Peter and his friends were fishing.

Reuben lowered the sail and rowed next to them. "That was quite a storm," he called.

"Yes, it kept us from going farther out," Peter called back.

"Have you caught anything?" Rueben asked.

"No," Peter answered, shaking his head. "But we're not ready to give up."

"Neither are we," Asher said, picking up his net.

Although, Benjamin and Gaspar were soaking wet, they grabbed their nets, too, and they began to cast them out. For the rest of the night, the two boats fished side by side, but the fish eluded their nets.

Toward morning, Benjamin's arms ached. He could barely move them, but he wouldn't quit. As the sun broke over the horizon, an orange glow rippled across the water. "It's daylight already and we have nothing to show for our labor," Asher grumbled.

Exhausted, Benjamin slumped to the bottom of the boat and closed his eyes. He longed for sleep.

"Look! It's Jesus!" Peter cried out.

Benjamin's eyes flew open. He sat up, putting his hand above his eyes to shade them from the sun.

Jesus was standing next to a glowing fire near the shore.

"Is that really Jesus?" Gaspar asked.

"Yes, He said He'd come, and He did." Benjamin's exhaustion evaporated instantly.

"Peter, lower your nets on the other side of the boat," Jesus called.

"We've fished all night and caught nothing, Master."

"Cast your nets out one more time."

Peter grabbed a net. "You heard Him. Do what He said."

The men in Peter's boat acted quickly. And without delay, Asher tossed his net out the other side of the boat. Benjamin and Gaspar followed his lead.

They watched and waited.

A few minutes later, Jesus called, "Haul them in."

They all pulled their nets in, and as they came over the side of the boat, the nets bulged with fish. On the deck, the nets burst open. Dozens of fish flopped around wildly on the bottom of the boat. Everyone scrambled to pitch the slippery catch into the straw baskets.

"I've never netted so many at one time," Peter shouted from his boat. To everyone's amazement, he jumped into the water and swam ashore. On land, he ran to Jesus and threw himself into His arms. Jesus laughed and embraced him.

When Jesus released Peter, He called, "Come ashore."

The boats headed in. Once they were docked, Peter hurried over to help unload the catch.

"Bring some fish to cook. We'll have a fine feast," Jesus said as he stood by the fire.

Benjamin carried a full basket off the boat, and he ran up the beach to where Jesus stood. His face was radiant. Benjamin put his basket down and scooped out two fish. With shaky hands, he gave them to Jesus.

"Benjamin, don't be afraid," Jesus said, smiling. "I've come to commission my Apostles to spread the news of my resurrection. As one who wants to be my disciple, you will be commissioned too. You will pass on to others what you have seen and heard."

"Am I really ready to become a disciple?"

Jesus nodded. "That's one of the reasons why I'm here."

A wide smile spread across Benjamin's face.

Jesus placed the fish Benjamin had given Him on sticks and leaned them over the fire that had been reduced to hot embers.

By now, the others had come up from their boats. Jesus embraced Andrew, James, and John. As soon as

He had finished, Benjamin said, "This is my friend, Gaspar, from Ethiopia."

Gaspar set down the basket of fish he held.

"I know about you, Gaspar. You have shown great love for your grandfather by coming to find me. On your return home, tell him that his generosity has never been forgotten. One day I will come and take him with me to share in my Father's kingdom."

Gaspar looked stunned as he stood still and silent.

Benjamin, unable to contain his excitement, asked, "What's the kingdom like?"

Jesus smiled. "There will be no more death, sorrow, or pain. This old world will pass away and everything will be made new."

"That sounds wonderful," Benjamin said. Then he turned to introduce Reuben and Asher, who were standing nearby. "Jesus, these are my cousins."

"Yes, Rueben and Asher are diligent fishermen who will one day become unwavering fishers of men."

"Fishers of men?" the two asked in unison.

Jesus laughed loudly. "You will find out more about that later. But right now, I would like to speak to Benjamin alone. Benjamin, would you walk with me?"

Why would Jesus want to talk to him in private? Benjamin shivered, but he fell into step with Jesus, and they walked together along the beach.

"Your mother's death caused you to become angry with God," Jesus said. "Your faith was shaken, but since receiving the gift of the Holy Spirit, God has restored your faith in Him."

Uncertain if he was ready to have his faith in God restored, Benjamin only nodded.

"Everything has a purpose. The purpose for your life will be revealed as you grow spiritually, and one day you will be reunited with your mother. She waits for you in Paradise."

Unable to hold onto his bitterness against God any longer, Benjamin took a deep breath and exhaled. He could feel his anger dissolve. He started to cry. Jesus stopped walking and embraced him. He held him until there were no tears left.

Benjamin wiped his sleeve across his wet face, and looking into Jesus' gentle eyes, he said, "How can I serve you? I once wanted to become a rabbi. Is that still possible now that I am to become a disciple?"

"All things are possible with God. Be patient with yourself. Your father taught you from the Torah. Trust what you have learned. I have not come to destroy the law but to fulfill it." Jesus paused, and then He said, "You have wanted to ask me a certain question for a long time. Ask it now."

Benjamin wasn't sure how to start so he just blurted it out, "If you are the Messiah, the one we have waited for all these years, why haven't you gathered an army to drive the Romans from our land?"

"I did not come to do battle. I came to tell of God's love for His people. When Adam and Eve sinned and left the garden of Paradise, the gates were closed behind them. God wants to draw His people back to Himself. My death removed sin and opened the gates again. Now that they are opened, all who believe in Me can enter into eternal life."

Benjamin nodded. "But there's still hatred and wars."

"That is true." Jesus nodded in agreement. "But when people allow the Holy Spirit to enter their lives, to teach and to guide them, hatred will no longer exist in their hearts or in their minds. They will learn to love one another. Benjamin, the Holy Spirit is with you always."

"Am I a disciple now?"

"Is that what you want?"

"More than anything!"

Jesus' eyes sparkled with laughter. "Yes, Benjamin, you are now one of my disciples."

The words sent shivers through Benjamin.

As they walked back to the fire, Benjamin felt as if he were floating. "Will I ever become an Apostle, like Peter?" he asked.

"There is only one Peter. You will come into your own and serve me faithfully. But remember," Jesus said gently, "the journey is not an easy one. You saw what they did to me in Jerusalem."

Benjamin grew serious for a moment, but then he smiled. "Yes, but I have the Holy Spirit with me always to guide me."

Jesus put an arm over Benjamin's shoulder. "Yes, you do. You certainly do."

TWENTY-THREE

COMMISSIONED

The mouthwatering smell of cooked fish filled the air. Everyone gathered around the fire waiting to eat. Reuben and Asher were exchanging fish stories with Andrew, James, and John.

Benjamin, next to Gaspar, couldn't stop smiling. He was finally one of Jesus' disciples.

Jesus knelt and placed pieces of the cooked fish on palm leaves. He handed them to Peter, who passed them around. Benjamin was given a leaf filled with fish. He quickly devoured one piece and started on another.

Jesus stood and added some wood to the fire. "I will go to my Father's kingdom to prepare a place for each of you," He said. "One day I will return to take you there."

Benjamin didn't want Jesus to leave. He didn't even want to think about it.

Jesus then turned and spoke to Peter, John, and Andrew. He was speaking so quietly that Benjamin couldn't hear what was being said. When He finished talking, Jesus walked with the Apostles to their boat. He embraced each of them as they got into their craft and pushed off.

Benjamin was puzzled. Why did they leave without saying goodbye?

He and Gaspar ate in silence. After Reuben and Asher finished their meal, Rueben said, "We're going to the boat to check on our nets. We'll be back as soon as we're done."

On their way, Jesus stopped them. They appeared to be listening intently to what He was saying. When He nodded at them, they left and continued to their boat.

Benjamin couldn't help wondering what Jesus had told them. He finished eating and tossed his palm leaf into the fire.

A sudden tap on his shoulder startled him. He turned, and to his amazement, the soldier, Marcus was standing behind him.

"What are you doing here?" Benjamin asked. His brow furrowed. "Did Thaddeus set you free?"

Marcus shook his head and pointed at a man standing by himself near the bottom of the path leading from the ridge. "That man snuck into camp where Thaddeus and his soldiers had stopped for the night. Once everyone was asleep, he set me free."

Benjamin squinted. "That's Barabbas! Why would he help you?"

"He was following your caravan at a distance. When I joined you at the Jordan, he thought we were friends.

Seeing Thaddeus shackle me and take me away made him angry. He followed them and rescued me. I knew you were coming here to find Jesus so we came too."

Just then, Jesus approached them. "Marcus, would you come with me? I would like to talk with you and Barabbas."

"You know my name?" Marcus asked in disbelief.

"He knows us all by name," Benjamin said, nodding.

Jesus and Marcus went over to where Barabbas stood. While they talked, Benjamin watched. Why hadn't he been included?

Then as if Jesus had again read Benjamin's thoughts, He called, "Come join us, Benjamin."

Looking at Gaspar, he didn't want leave his friend alone. But Gaspar smiled as if he understood. "Go, he's calling you. It must be important."

When Benjamin reached them, Jesus said, "Marcus and Barabbas have something they need to tell you."

Barabbas' eyes no longer looked troubled. He seemed at peace. "Marcus didn't mean to stab your mother," he said. "I was the one he wanted to kill that day in the marketplace. At that time we were enemies."

Marcus traced the scar on his face. "As a youth, my father taught me to wield a sword. On purpose, he cut me with his. He told me he did it to teach me to defend myself and make me a brave warrior. Instead, I learned to hate my father's cruel ways. And I began to hurt others as he had hurt me."

Benjamin stared at Marcus' scar. It must have been awful to not to have known a father's love. What if

Benjamin hadn't known the kindness of his parents? How would he act toward others?

"Jesus explained to me about forgiveness," Marcus continued. "He forgave me for my brutal treatment of the Jews, and I've forgiven my father for his cruelty. Benjamin, can you let go of your hatred for me? Can you find it in your heart to forgive me for your mother's death? I'm so sorry for what has happened." Marcus' eyes were wet with tears.

Benjamin's eyes were watery too. He was quick to wipe them with his sleeve. Now that he was a disciple, he wanted to follow what Jesus had said earlier: "Love God and your neighbor as yourself."

Benjamin felt his anger dissipate and a feeling of peace washed over him. Finally, he said, "Marcus, I do forgive you."

A wide smile spread across Marcus' face. "That means more to me than you can imagine."

"Benjamin," Jesus said, "Marcus told me he entrusted his sword to you. The sword is mighty, but words of love and forgiveness speak more powerfully than any weapon. Spoken in anger, words can kill a person's spirit. Whereas, words of encouragement can heal a broken heart. Each of you has shown an eagerness to be my disciple. You will go forth to tell others about your experiences with me. Truth is the weapon you will wield."

"Do you still have the sword?" Marcus asked.

Benjamin nodded and ran to the pile of rocks where

he had it hidden. He returned carrying the brass belt and the encased sword. He handed them to Marcus.

Marcus waved them away. "I have no use for them anymore."

"Place them on the fire," Jesus said.

Benjamin dropped them onto the embers. To his surprise, the belt and sheath burst into flames, sending black smoke billowed into the air. The sword's metal blade melted like wax.

A soft wind swirled around the fire, and out of the blaze fluttered a pure white dove. It hovered above the flames for a moment before flying off across the water.

As it soared out of sight, Benjamin smiled. "I feel as if I've been set free! Free to soar as a bird!"

"Me too," Marcus said, grinning.

Even Barabbas was smiling beneath his shabby beard.

Marcus placed his hand on Benjamin's shoulder. "Someday our paths will cross again, but for now, Barabbas and I will travel the back roads, spreading Jesus' message of God's love and forgiveness to all."

After they said their goodbyes, Marcus and Barabbas hiked up the long winding path and disappeared over the ridge.

"Will there ever come a time when peace exists between the Jews and Romans?" Benjamin asked Jesus.

"Seek the peace that is inside you. Share what you find with everyone you meet, no matter who they are. We all need friends, even me."

"Could I be your friend?"

Jesus placed His pierced hands over Benjamin's.

"You are my friend, but sometimes, friends must go their separate ways, even if they don't want to."

"You're leaving?"

"Yes, but I promise I'll come back for you."

Jesus called Gaspar to join them. "You are returning home soon?" He asked.

"Yes, my grandfather's been waiting a long time to hear the news about you and your kingdom. As soon as I get my camel, Ade, from the elderly gentleman who borrowed him, I'll leave."

"Peter will stay in Tiberias until the end of the month," Jesus said. "Then he will travel back to Jerusalem. When are you going home, Benjamin?"

"I told Grandfather I'd be home for the harvest."

"Would you like to make the journey back with Peter?"

"Yes, if my cousin Isaac can come too. He's going to work in the olive grove with my grandfather and me. And in the evening, we're to study the Torah together."

"It's settled. I have talked with Peter. He will meet you here the day after tomorrow if you still want to fish. But if you have had enough fishing, he said he knows where your uncle lives. He will come for you and Isaac at month's end. They left now because they wanted time to spend with their families before they return to Jerusalem."

Jesus embraced Gaspar. When He hugged Benjamin, He whispered, "Remember all I have told you." He released His hold, and then made His way to the water's edge where He stood for a moment looking into the sky. Benjamin watched as Jesus walked down the beach and His figure faded into the morning sunlight.

Although he knew that he would see Jesus again, still, sadness swept over him.

"Come on you two, we'd better leave. Mother will wonder why we're so late." It was Asher, he and Reuben had come up from their boat carrying baskets of fish.

"I'm ready," Benjamin said, lifting his basket to his shoulder.

Gaspar picked his up too.

Asher scratched his head, "We've had quite a time. Something I'll never forget."

Benjamin nodded as he and Gaspar fell into step behind his cousins. "Your grandfather was right, Gaspar. He knew Jesus would be a great King, although His kingdom is not of this world. I can hardly wait to tell Rachel and Daniel all the things that have happened since leaving home!"

"Who are Daniel and Rachel?"

"They are my friends from home."

They walked along in silence, each lost in their own thoughts until they reached the large limestone house set back from the road.

"Father, Mother, we're home," Asher called.

Uncle Solomon rushed outside. "Your baskets are full. How did you get such a large catch?"

"We'll explain it later while we eat," Reuben said.

"Your mother will like that. She has been anxiously awaiting your return. But I have something to show Benjamin first."

While the others went inside, Benjamin left his basket by the door and followed Uncle Solomon to the back of the house. In the middle of a group of fruit trees was a dogwood tree in full bloom. "Uncle, this tree is like the one cut down by the guards."

"Yes, it's the same as your grandfather's."

Benjamin gently touched one of the cream-colored blossoms. "May I take a sprig home for him?"

"We'll cut one the day you leave. But since the aroma of your aunt's freshly baked bread has been tempting me all morning, let's go and eat." Uncle Solomon headed to the house.

Benjamin smiled and in spite of his full stomach, he didn't hesitate to follow his uncle. He always had room for Aunt Esther's warm bread.

At the front door, Uncle Solomon said, "God has blessed this house abundantly with our family, our friends, and plenty of food." He picked up the basket of fish Benjamin had left at the door and went inside.

Benjamin stood there a minute alone and the sacred words he thought he would never say again crossed his lips, "Hear O Israel! The Lord is our God, the Lord is one! You shall love the Lord your God with all your heart, and with all your soul, and with all your might. These words, which I am commanding you today shall be on your heart."

He realized the prayer he spoke was now sealed in his heart forever.

The End

ABOUT THE AUTHOR

Caye Patterson Bartell changed how she viewed herself as a writer when at a Christian Writers Conference, she discovered that writing could also be a ministry. Her awareness of God in each ordinary day showed up in her poems, short stories, and devotionals. After her second pilgrimage to Israel, she felt inspired to write a novel set in the Holy Lands during the time of Jesus. Her journey while writing this book not only enriched her personal relationship with the Lord, but it also increased her knowledge of the Holy Spirit's guidance, and it taught her to let go of her own plans and to trust in God.